# 어느 피씨주의자의 종생기

〈K-픽션〉 시리즈는 한국문학의 젊은 상상력입니다. 최근 발표된 가장 우수하고 흥미로운 작품을 엄선하여 출간하는 〈K-픽션〉은 한국문학의 생생한 현장을 국내외 독자들과 실시간으로 공유하고자 기획되었습니다. 〈바이링궐 에디션 한국 대표 소설〉 시리즈를 통해 검증된 탁월한 번역진이 참여하여 원작의 재미와 품격을 최대한 살린 〈K-픽션〉 시리즈는 매 계절마다 새로운 작품을 선보입니다.

The K-Fiction Series represents the brightest of young imaginative voices in contemporary Korean fiction. This series consists of a wide range of outstanding contemporary Korean short stories that the editorial board of *ASIA* carefully selects each season. These stories are then translated by professional Korean literature translators, all of whom take special care to faithfully convey the pieceså original tones and grace. We hope that, each and every season, these exceptional young Korean voices will delight and challenge all of you, our treasured readers both here and abroad.

K-Fiction Series

# 어느 피씨주의자의 종생기
## The Story of P.C.

구병모 | 스텔라 김 옮김
Written by Gu Byeong-mo
Translated by Stella Kim

ASIA
PUBLISHERS

차례

Contents

# 어느 피씨주의자의 종생기

The Story of P.C.

소설가 P씨의 계정을 팔로우한 지는 2년 남짓 되었다. P씨의 팔로워는 5만여 명인데 팔로잉은 3명에 불과했으며, 그것은 친구나 가족이 아니라 지금까지 그의 책을 출간한 출판사들의 계정이었다. 그는 1년에 평균 1권꼴로 6년째 저서를 출간했는데 모두 소설이었고 웬만큼 쓴다는 작가라면 으레 한 권쯤 낼 법도 한 산문집은 없었다. 그러고 보면 P씨는 신문, 잡지, 방송 어디에도 칼럼을 신는 법이 없었다. 생활 밀착형 미셀러니를 비롯하여 무게감 있는 에세이나 사회·문화 논평에 이르기까지, 말하자면 소설 아닌 글은 무엇 하나 발표하지 않았다. 소설은 인물이나 줄거리 따라가는 재미에

I started following P.C.'s Twitter account about two years ago. P.C. was a novelist who had over 50,000 followers, but who followed only three Twitter accounts, none of which were those of friends or family, but instead publishers of his or her books. For the past six years, this writer had published an average of one book per year—all fiction. P.C. didn't even have a collection of essays, which so many writers publish after a few novels. Come to think of it, P.C. also never wrote columns for newspaper or magazines, or appeared on TV shows. No casual pieces about their life or more serious essays or social and cultural commentaries —P.C. wrote nothing but fiction.

집중하느라 티가 잘 나지 않지만, 스토리텔링이 적은 산문에서는 저자의 평소 사고와 문장의 밑천이 드러나게 마련이었다. 그가 평소 SNS에 올리는 토막 단상들은 그럴듯한 삽화를 얹어 책으로 대강 엮어 팔기에 큰 무리는 없지만 범상한 문장만큼이나 사유 또한 단순하여 지나가는 누구를 붙잡고 물어도 그 정도 말은 구사할 수 있겠다 싶은, 말하자면 저자 특유의 개성이 드러나지 않는 글이었으니, 산문집을 굳이 출간하지 않는 것은 암만 수익지상주의 업체라도 최소한의 보는 눈 내지는 출판의 사회적 책무를 고려하는 양심이 있다는 뜻이며, 이 세상의 푸르른 나무들을 위해서도 올바른 선택일 터였다.

딱히 내세울 것 없는 문체와 살짝 빈곤한 사유에도 불구하고 P씨가 매해 꼬박 신간을 선보이며 꾸준한 판매 지수를 유지하는 한편 웹에서는 수많은 팔로워를 거느린 까닭이라면 역시 그거지. 첫 책이 16부작 케이블 드라마로, 두 번째가 영화로, 세 번째가 20회작 웹드라마로. 진정한 의미에서의 대박은 첫 번째뿐이며 작품이 유명세를 탔다고 하여 그걸 쓴 작가가 셀러브리티는 아니겠으나, 이후 꾸준한 중박으로 업계 입장에서는 뭘

Fiction tends to be driven by characters and plots, of course, while essays, which involve less storytelling, can reveal a writer's thoughts in a different way. It's true that snippets of P.C.'s thoughts posted on Twitter were good enough to be bound into a book, with illustrations. But they were generally mediocre writings, based on simple ideas that anyone on the street might have. They didn't contain characteristics unique to the author. Therefore, the fact that P.C. didn't publish a collection of essays seemed to suggest that the writer's publishers, despite their profit-seeking nature, were ethical enough to honor the social responsibility of publishing, or, at the very least, could distinguish good writing from bad. It certainly was the right thing to do—even for the green trees of this world.

Despite their ordinary writing style and rather mediocre ideas, a new book by P.C. was released every year, recorded steady sales, and maintained a sizable following. How was that so? It was possible because P.C.'s first book was turned into a 16-episode TV drama series on a cable network. The second became a film, and the third was made into an online-only drama series with 20 episodes. Only the first book could be considered a true "hit,"

해도 본전치기는 하겠다 싶은 작가가 그리 흔치 않지. 원소스멀티유즈가 가능한 몇 안 되는 작가 중 하나, 계산기 두드려봤을 때 손해는 안 나고 언젠가 다시 터질 잭팟에 대한 기대를 완전히 접을 필요도 없는 고른 작품 수준—알다시피 우리가 대형마트 팝업보드나 식당 메뉴판에서 종종 발견하는 '고른 품질' 내지는 '균질한 맛' 따위의 표현은 딱 가성비라든가 그보다 살짝 밑도는, 하여간 그리 큰 기대를 하지 않는 편이 좋다는 뜻이다—거기에 얼굴을 드러내지 않고 인터뷰에도 응하지 않음으로써 본명과 성별 및 나이와 직업, 거주지 등 정체를 궁금하게 만드는 은둔자 이미지도 한몫할 터다.

매년 발표하는 소설마다 소비되기 좋고 소진되기도 쉬운 적당한 감흥을 안겨주는 P씨의 계정을 처음 팔로우한 이유는, 마침 그 무렵 논란이 된 사례에 대해 P씨가 어떻게 대처하는지 보려고—그보다는 이런 논란을 일으키는 사람의 일상을, 그의 토막글과 사진만으로 어디까지 파악할 수 있을지 호기심이 생겨서였다고 할 것이다.

당시 P씨가 발표한 신작은 그전까지 재개발 구역의 휴먼코미디-병원 배경의 미스터리 로맨스-고등학교

though, and the fact that the drama series was popular did not necessarily make its writer a celebrity. Nevertheless, P.C.'s later works were mildly successful, and not many writers' works allowed publishers to break even. As it turned out, P.C. was one of the few writers whose books could be turned into other media, the publishers knew they weren't going to lose money, and they didn't need to give up on a vision of P.C.'s books someday hitting the jackpot. What's more, the quality of the author's work was even—not top-quality, name-brand, but good generic brands—not bad, for their cost; people didn't expect much besides what they were getting. On top of that, P.C. never appeared in public or agreed to do an interview. Since no one knew P.C.'s real name, sex, age, occupation, or address, the mysterious image created a kind of appeal for the readers.

The reason I decided to follow P.C. on social media—a writer who every year published a book that piqued just enough interest to be widely consumed, and then faded in people's memories—was that I wanted to see how he or she would respond to the controversy that arose at the time—or, rather, because I was curious to find out how far I could glimpse, from snippets of writings and pic-

신임교사의 참교육 도전기 등으로 이어져온 일련의 소설에서 따뜻하고 푹신한 톤을 덜어낸 것으로, 소위 사회파 스릴러로 분류할 수 있는 내용이었다. 이때 주인공을 통해 선악의 모호한 경계를 성공적으로 형상화했다는 북섹션 리뷰와 함께, 기존 그의 작품들이 거쳐온 수순대로 영화사에서 수시로 접촉이 들어온다는 보도가 뒤따랐다. 그런데 인물들을 하나씩 톺아보면, 주인공 옆에 상당한 비중으로 다루어지는 악인은 불법체류 중인 외국인 노동자였고, 그 외에 시골 총각과 결혼한 지 한 달 만에 가산을 돌라내어 도망가다 잡히자 배 째라고 내미는 방글라데시 여인에다, 주인공의 보조자로 미모의 청각장애인이 등장했다. 도대체 인물만 열거해서는 무슨 이야기인지 알 수 없을 법한 소설이라는 점은 접어두고, 350여 쪽의 책에서 열두 개 문단 정도가 캡처 편집되어 서브컬처 게시판에 올라가자 아직 책을 접하지 않은 이들은 그 편협함과 낡은 세계관에 경악했고, 이미 책을 읽은 이들은 스스로 둔감했음을 한탄했다. 나는 그때까지 누구에게 선물로 줄까 말까 고민하면서 그 책을 3부 정도 장바구니에만 담았다가, 끝내 결제 버튼을 클릭하지 않고 이듬해 보관함으로 이동시켰다.

tures posted, the life of a person who had created such a controversy.

P.C.'s new novel was different from earlier ones, which included a comedy set at the site of an urban redevelopment project, a mystery-romance in a hospital, and a story about a new high-school teacher who wanted to make a difference in the world. The latest novel lacked the warmth and softness of the earlier works though: you might call it a social thriller. A review in a newspaper's book section mentioned the writer's successful depiction, through the main character, of the blurry line between good and evil. That review was soon followed by articles revealing how film producers were busy contacting P.C.'s publisher about turning the novel into a film, as they had done with the author's previous works.

Yet a closer inspection of the characters in the novel by some people revealed problems. The villain—as prominent a character as the protagonist—was an illegal immigrant. A Bangladeshi woman who had married a farmer tried to run away with his money a month after the wedding. When caught, she shamelessly challenged him: "Sue me!" And a beautiful woman with a hearing impairment acted as the protagonist's sidekick.

게시판에서 SNS로 이동한 편집본이 리트윗 단계로 넘어가자, P씨의 소설은 외국인 노동자가 악인이라는 편견을 고착화하여 기피 대상으로 규정하는 데에 한몫하며, 매매혼이나 다름없는 현 사회의 뒤틀린 국제결혼 문화에 대한 반성과 고찰 없이 외국인 신부를 사기꾼으로 몰아간 데다 그녀의 서툰 한국어를 지속적으로 드러내어 희화화하는 한편, 선한 행동에서 성스러운 느낌마저 자아내는 청각장애인 여성이 주인공의 보조자에 그침으로써 장애인은 모두 착하고 순박해야 마땅한 사람들이라는 고정관념—강요된 이미지를 재생산 및 배포하는 이야기가 되었다. 특히 주인공이 제 분을 못 이기고 그녀에게 '병신'이나 '귀머거리'라고 반복적으로 토해내는 장면은 해당 인물의 내적 갈등을 보여주는 장치로 기능하기보다는 청각장애인에 대한 잘못된 인식과 명칭을 공고히 하며, 설령 그것이 주인공의 내적 갈등을 형상화하기 위한 장면이라고 주장한들, 반드시 한 주체의 인격을 짓밟음으로써 갈등을 표현할 수밖에 없다면 작가의 소양이 저급하다는 뜻이라는 사람들의 분석이 이어졌다. 주인공의 폭언을 듣지 못하나 입모양과 행동으로 무슨 뜻인지 알아차린 여성이 분노하기는커녕 그

Aside from the fact that these characters did not give the faintest clues about the story itself, when about a dozen paragraphs from this 350-page novel were posted on an online message board of a subculture website, people were appalled by the author's prejudices and old-fashioned worldview, while those who had actually read the book lamented their own insensitivity to such matters. At the time, I had just put three copies of the book in my shopping cart at a bookseller's website, thinking I might give them to people as gifts; but instead of purchasing them, I moved them to my "save for later" list in the following year.

When an edited version of the post on that website made its way into the wider social media, and began to be retweeted, P.C.'s latest novel had become a story that personified the stereotype of illegal immigrants as criminals and people who should be shunned. Also, it portrayed a foreign-born bride as a criminal, without reflecting on the current problem of international marriages as a form of human trafficking, while at the same time it ridiculed her poor command of Korean. And it limited the role of a hearing-impaired woman (whose actions were purely good to the point of being saint-like) to being his mere helper, thereby reproducing and

를 포옹하는 장면은 모성 판타지의 일종이겠는데, 이때 그녀가 하필이면 날씬하고 아름다운 여성이라는 사전 묘사는 각종 혐의에 화룡정점을 찍었다. 고작 한 권의 소설에서 이렇게 용납하기 어려운 대목이 쏟아져 나온다는 건 그 저자가 평소 어떤 가치관을 지녔는지를 보여준다는 댓글과 타래들이 달렸다.

문제가 불거지고 일주일 넘게 P씨는 자신의 SNS에 글을 올리지 않아서, 사람들은 그가 접속을 자주 하지 않는 것으로 여겼다. 그도 그럴 것이 그는 평소 자신의 정치적 신념이 드러날 만한 외신 기사 한 토막을 리트윗하는 손가락조차 매우 인색했으며, 대부분은 사진과 함께 있어도 없어도 그만이며 자기 건지 누구 건지 모를 사색을 포함하여 때론 저자가 명시된 시나 소설의 일부를 인용하여 올리는 정도로 가뭄에 콩 나듯 활동을 유지하고 있었다. P씨의 저서는 그때그때 출판사 계정에서 알아서 홍보했고 그 자신은 신간이 나왔다거나 이번에도 잘 부탁드린다든지 같은, 개인 육성이 드러나는 말 한마디를 보태지 않았다. 팔로워가 책을 잘 읽었다든가 앞으로도 꾸준한 활동을 부탁드린다고 말을 걸면 웃음 이모티콘에 Thank you가 적힌 이미지로만 답글

spreading the prejudicial image of individuals with disabilities as necessarily always kind and innocent.

People claimed that the scenes in which the protagonist, unable to control himself, yelled at his helper, sometimes even calling her "cripple" or "deaf," rather than functioning as a mechanism for revealing the protagonist's inner conflicts, were furthering misconceptions about and the use of reprehensible terms for people with impairments. Furthermore, people argued that even if the author were to assert that this behavior was a means for expressing the protagonist's inner conflicts, doing so by trampling on another person's dignity was proof of the writer's crude and uncultured perspective.

There were scenes in which the helper could not hear the protagonist yelling and swearing, but understood what he was saying by reading his lips and his actions, yet she still embraced him, instead of angrily denouncing him. This was to be understood as a kind of maternal fantasy; but the description of her as slender and beautiful poured gas on the already-blazing controversy. The fact that such a flood of unacceptable ideas was gushing from a single book, people said, revealed the author's skewed values.

을 보내는데, 무성의하다는 지적을 피하기 위해서인지 Thank you 문구만 고정이고 배경 이미지는 매번 다양한 사진과 그림을 사용했으며, 악플이나 시비 거는 말에는 대꾸하지 않았다. 따라서 그동안에도 이렇게 소극적으로 소통할 거면 애당초 자물쇠를 채우거나 익명으로 할 일이지 뭐하러 P씨라는 이름으로 공개 계정을 팠느냐는 불평과 비판이 종종 있었다.

이대로 사안이 묻히게 두고 볼 수 없었던 유저들은 작가가 먼저 입을 열지 않으니 출판사 계정에 지속적 멘션을 보내서 해명과 이후 방침을 요구하기 시작했는데, 그런 다음 올라온 P씨의 첫 게시물은 놀랍게도 카메라의 제원만 밝혔을 뿐 별다른 캡션이 없는 사진 세 장이었다.

물론 그전에도 P씨는 설명 없이 직접 찍었다고 추정되는 사진들을 종종 올렸고, 사진에는 그 자신이나 주변 지인으로 추정되는 인물은 전혀 없이 주로 자연 풍경, 국내외의 거리 모습과 타인임이 분명한 사람들, 박물관이나 전시관을 비롯한 어떤 장소와 정물을 비롯한 인테리어가 나타나 있었다. 사람들은 그 대중없는 이미지의 파편들을 조합하여 그가 어느 지역에 사는지 어떤

For over a week after the controversy erupted, P.C. didn't upload a single post on Twitter, which led people to believe that he seldom checked the social media account. It seemed to be true, too, since P.C. rarely, if ever, retweeted even a short article from a foreign newspaper that might reveal his or her own political stance, and once in a blue moon, P.C. posted photographs with general thoughts or ideas, which could be the author's own but also might not, and snippets of poems or stories along with the name of the poet or writer. When P.C.'s works were published, although the publishers promoted them, P.C. never commented on them, never announced the publication of new works, nor asked people to buy or read them. When P.C.'s followers tweeted him, saying that they enjoyed a book and hoped that he would continue to write, P.C. simply answered with "Thank you" and a smiley emoji. And, possibly wanting to avoid seeming insincere, P.C. used different background images for replies and never commented on malicious tweets or argumentative remarks. So, even before the controversy over that new book, the writer's followers had occasionally complained and criticized him for having a public social media account when he clearly did not wish to communicate.

곳을 여행하고 어디에 들렀으며 무슨 종류의 문화생활을 영위하고 관심사가 무엇인지를 추측하는 한편, 그렇게 드러난 관심사를 통해 성별과 나이와 가족 사항을 분석하기도 했다. 화면 구도 잡는 방식이 거칠고 대범하며 아기자기한 소품에는 관심이 없는 한편, 분위기 좋은 이탈리안 레스토랑에 몇 번이나 가놓고도 테이블의 음식 사진이 단 한 번도 올라오지 않았고 평소 고양이나 강아지 사진이 전무한데, 서로 다른 디지털카메라의 스펙을 비교하는 장면이나 무언가를 분해하고 조립하는 장면이 종종 올라온 것으로 보아서 안정적 수입원이 있는 남성일 확률이 높다든가, 아니 굳이 사진으로 판단할 거 없이 이미 발표한 소설마다 매번 30대 중반의 남성이 중심 화자라는 사실만으로도 알조라거나, 일상생활 관련 성토 내지는 푸념이 엿보이지 않으며 수많은 미술관과 여행지 사진으로 보아선 결혼하지 않았거나 최소한 자녀가 없는 우아하고 윤택하며 기품 있는 생활을 누리고 있으리라는 추측, 어딘지 모를 초등학교 운동회 장면이 최소한의 연출과 구도를 무시한 채 올라온 걸 보면 아이를 둔 부모라는 또 다른 추측, 그 정도야 단지 지나가다 찍은 풍경일 수 있다는 반론, 아니 확실

Since P.C. was not responding to the controversy, those Internet users who could not stand to see the controversy buried continued to tweet the publisher, demanding an explanation for P.C.'s new book and the publisher's plan to deal with it. To everyone's surprise, the first posts that popped up on P.C.'s social media account a few days later were three pictures with captions specifying the camera models used to take them.

It's true that P.C. had occasionally posted pictures that he or she had taken, usually without captions or descriptions, and none of the images were of the author or possible. acquaintances. Mainly, they were of nature, streets in different countries and people who were clearly strangers, museums, and exhibitions; indeed, their only common quality was that they captured certain places, things, or interiors. Nevertheless, people joined together those inconsistent and fragmented images and used them to make conjectures about the place P.C. lived, the sites he visited, the type of cultural activities the writer enjoyed, his interests and hobbies. Citing evidence they had collected, some went as far as trying to deduce P.C.'s gender, age, and family relations. Based on facts like: the composition of the photographs that P.C. tweeted tended to be bold

히 일련의 다른 사진들에 비해 소재가 이질적일 뿐만 아니라 결이 달라 결이, 뭐가 됐든 사진과 글을 주로 올리는 시각으로 볼 때 회사원은 아니고 자영업자겠지, 아니 자영업 하면서 가게 놔두고 이렇게 많은 곳을 돌아다닐 수 있나, 결론은 프리랜서나 전업작가, 그런데 포털 연재도 아닌 연 1권 전작 출간만으로 먹고살 수 있는 전업작가가 우리나라에 몇 명이나 되겠으며, 매번 영화나 드라마의 2차 판권료를 억대로 받지 않고서야 불가능하지 않나, SNS에 비교 분석기가 올라온 그의 카메라를 보자면 렌즈 포함 오백만 원에 이르니 애당초 돈 좀 있는 딜레탕트이겠다든가, 아니면 또 다른 필명으로 대중성 있고 접근성 좋은 플랫폼에 좀 더 로맨틱하거나 에로틱하거나 속도감 넘치는 무언가를 연재하여 생계를 메울지도…… 같은 식이었다.

그러나 그전까지의 짐작이 일종의 유희 차원에서 오간 이야기였다면, 이번 경우는 P씨 자신과 직접 관련된 일이 벌어지는 중인데 관련 피드백 없이 파도가 덮쳐오는 찰나를 찍은 사진만 올리다니, 책을 내놓고 나 몰라라 하는 무책임이 도를 넘어 독자를 무시하는 처사가 아니냐는 비난이 높아졌다.

and rough, he didn't seem interested in cute little things, there were pictures of upscale Italian restaurants, yet not a single picture of food on a table, there were no pictures of cats or dogs, and P.C. occasionally posted images comparing the specifications of different digital cameras or assembled or dissembled products, some people claimed there was a strong possibility that P.C. was a man, one with a stable income. Others countered that there was no need to analyze the pictures posted on P.C.'s social media account, since the fact that the narrators of his novels were men in their mid-30s made it obvious that the author was similar. Still others hypothesized that P.C. led an elegant and luxurious life, unmarried, or at least without children, considering the lack of complaints or grievances about having to endure the daily grind, as well as an abundance of photographs of art museums and travel. Yet others guessed that P.C. was a parent with children, citing a picture of a field day at a school taken without any particular composition or direction; while others refuted the argument because those images could have been captured in passing by. But then, no: the subject of the photograph was nothing like other ones P.C. posted, and the texture, oh, the texture, was very different...

그러자 재차 해명을 요청하는 목소리가 나오는 막간을 틈타, P씨의 첫 책부터 의심스러운 대목이 깻단 속 낟알처럼 털려 나오기 시작했다. 재개발 구역을 무대로 한 첫 번째 책에서는, 이미 반쯤 헐려 벽 너머가 드러난 집에서 맘에 두고 있던 여성과 다른 남성이 관계하는 모습을 목격한 주인공이 그쪽에 대고 소변을 발사하는 장면이나, 우연히 이 소변 줄기를 맞은 길고양이를 학대 살해하는 행위가 적나라하게 묘사된 장면이 문제로 꼽혔으며 이 묘사만 떠낸 이미지는 동물사랑협회 관계자들에 의해 대거 리트윗되었다. 케이블드라마에서는 이 부분이 최대한 각색 편집되어, 빈집의 성관계는 방송 매체라는 특성상 등장하지도 않았고 소변 맞은 고양이는 오히려 주인공을 할퀴고 도망가는 장면으로 처리되었으며 이때 대놓고 코믹한 배경음악이 깔렸는데, 드라마만 보았던 대부분의 사람들은 뒤늦게 원작 소설의 해당 대목을 보고 경악했다. 소설 속 고양이가 다루어진 방식이 오래전 에드거 앨런 포의 플루토는 저리 가라인데 그것이 인간에게 내재한 본질적 악을 환기하는 공포의 미학보다는 혐오와 불쾌감을 유발하니 선정적이고 저급한 수준에 불과하다는 보충 멘션이 달리는 동

Whatever it was, considering the uploaded pictures and posts, P.C. probably had his or her own business. What, can someone who owns a business go traveling so much? So people concluded that P.C. must be a freelancer or a full-time writer; but how many full-time writers in Korea make a living off a book a year, without writing serially on websites, and wouldn't such a life be impossible unless P.C. received huge amounts of money for the rights to films and dramas based on his novels? Some compared the cameras that P.C. owned with high-end ones and commented that since the camera and the lenses cost five million won, P.C. was probably a rich dilettante. Others speculated that the writer might be making a living by composing something more romantic or erotic or fast-paced on popular websites under a different pseudonym.

People had made such conjectures about P.C. for their own entertainment before the controversy; but now the criticisms mounted over his posting pictures of crashing waves without saying a word about the controversy over the new book. Clearly, P.C. had gone too far in writing such a questionable book, ignoring readers, and taking no responsibility for the ensuing controversy.

As some people continued to demand an expla-

안, 사면을 가리지도 못한 집에서 성관계를 맺은 동네 여성의 생리적 수치심은 상대적으로 덜 부각되었을 정도였다. 두 번째 소설의 배경인 병원에서는 30대 후반의 수간호사가 의사와, 20대 후반의 간호사가 담당 환자와 불륜에 빠지는데 각 장면과 상황이 고요한 분위기로 에로티시즘의 기름기를 쏙 빼고 그려지자 오히려 수채화 같은 풍경이 연출되는 바람에 불륜을 미화할뿐더러 사명감으로 고된 노동을 버티는 간호사 집단을 모욕한다는 판결을 받았으며, 특히 의사의 가족과 환자의 가족에게 이입한 가정충실주의자들의 공분을 사는 한편, 의사와 환자가 결국 각자의 가정으로 돌아가 연착륙했는데 불륜을 저지른 자들이 그리 손쉽게 면죄부를 받아서는 안 된다는 주장이 뒤따랐다. 거기에 전현직 간호사를 칭하는 일련의 무리가 뜨더귀판에 참전하여, 종합병원 급의 간호사는 결혼이나 임신 차례까지 정해주는 3교대에 연애할 시간은커녕 기초적 가정생활도 건사하기 힘들어 끝내 퇴직하는 경우가 적지 않을뿐더러, 설령 의사와 연애를 한대도 그것은 상하 수직관계에서 발생하는 권력에 마지못해 끌려간 겁박의 일종일 가능성이 크고, 한편 피고름과 토사물 등의 감염 위험

nation about his new book, others began combing through the author's earlier works and posted all the supposedly questionable parts. In the first novel, set in an area designated for urban development, the protagonist witnesses the woman he loves having sex with another man in a house that is half torn down, urinates in their direction, and then abuses and kills a cat splashed by his urine. The graphic descriptions of these scenes came to the fore, and animal rights organizations rushed to retweet the description. In the cable drama adapted from the book, these scenes had been edited and revised in consideration of the age-rating restrictions; the sex scene wasn't even included, and the scene with the cat was completely changed: the urine-spattered animal simply scratched the protagonist and ran away, with comical sounds playing in the background. Since most people had only watched the drama, they were appalled to learn of the original scenes in the book. The treatment of the cat was considered much worse than how the black cat, Pluto, was treated in Edgar Allan Poe's short story, since instead of the aesthetics of fear bringing to mind the fundamental evil inherent in humans, this depiction had only created hate and discomfort, which clearly revealed how P.C.'s

물을 삼시세끼처럼 마주하며 소변줄 등의 교체 과정에서 오랫동안 씻지 못한 아랫도리를 보게 되는 입원환자와의 사이에 연애감정이 성립하기도 어려운 현실이니, 그저 환상과 낭만에 의존한 작가의 조사가 얼마나 부실했는지를 보여주는 증거라 못 박기도 했다. 세 번째는 교사의 서사와 병행하여 움직이는 중심축의 고등학생 두 명이 모두 강인하고 순수하여, 어른들이 요구하는 프레임을 씌운 소위 대견한 청소년들로 묘사된다는 점에서 올드한 교훈주의라는 얘기가 나왔다. 공교롭게도 그 세 권의 소설은 모두 우리 집에 있었고……

특히 세 번째 책 같은 경우는 당시 전형적 힐링물로 평가받기도 해서, 자녀 교육 문제에 관심 있는 주위 엄마들에게 몇 권이나 선물로 돌렸었다. 그 뒤 교내 봉사활동 모임 후 커피숍에서 만난 엄마들의 감상평이 대략 어땠는가 하면, 자신의 딸과 아들이 꼭 그 주인공들처럼 자랐으면 싶은 바람과, 그럼에도 불구하고 소설 속에서 아이들이 좌충우돌하는 교사를 돕다가 겪은 각종 환난을 생각해볼 때, 가능하면 튀지 않고 조용히 수행평가와 입시에 전념했으면 좋겠다는 염려가 공존한다는 상식적·보편적 차원의 것이었다. 그중 한 엄마는, 그

treatment of the ca in the novel was excessively savage. Comments about this scene kept flooding social media, to the point that the outrage surrounding the embarrassment and shame the woman must have felt in the sex scene, exposed in a house without walls, was relatively less pronounced.

P.C.'s second novel, which was set in a hospital, featured two affairs: one between a head nurse in her late 30s and a married doctor, the other between a nurse in her late 20s and a patient. They were depicted as pure and romantic love stories, like a watercolor painting, without the excess of eroticism, which came into the line of fire as people decided that the novel romanticized affairs and insulted nurses, who had to perform intensive labor with a sense of commitment. The novel also angered devoted family men and women, who identified with the wives and children of the married doctor and the patient, characters who later returned to their families—which led to yet another thread about how people involved in affairs should not be easily forgiven and accepted back. Then a group of former and active nurses marched into this battle of words to explain that nurses working at general hospitals barely had time for their own

상황에서 아이들이 어떻게 자신감을 잃지 않고 갈등을 일소에 해소하면서 큰 방황 없이 올바른 인간으로서의 선택을 할 수 있었는지 모르겠다며, 자신은 성공적 인물 형상화의 첫 번째 요건이 입체성에 있다고 여기는 만큼, 작가가 세계를 바라보는 시각이 평면적이고 나이브한 것 같다고 첨언했다. 그러자 다른 엄마는, 고작 극적 구성을 위해 아이들이 크게 잘못된 길에 빠졌다가 올바른 길로 돌아오는 것이 오히려 나태하거나 개연성 없게 여겨진다면서, 처음부터 맑았던 아이들이 큰 굴곡 없이 끝까지 맑다는 점이야말로 이 소설의 특색이자 강점이라고 꼽았다. 그러자 또 다른 엄마는 문학의 결말에서 주인공들이 항상 올바른 길로 돌아와야 한다는 법은 없다고 말했고 마지막 엄마는, 그러면 남은 선택지라곤 처음부터 탁했던 아이들이 끝까지 탁한 인간으로 남는 것뿐인데 혹시 소설 속 아이들이 파멸하기를 바랐던 거냐고 반문하면서, 이 소설은 인물들이 정규교육을 받는 고교생들이라는 점에서 학교 밖 청소년들에 대한 교육과 돌봄을 배제한 반쪽짜리라 말했다. 그들이 문제의 원인을 제공한 내 쪽으로 고개를 돌리더니 너는 어느 쪽이냐고 묻기에, 나는 어려운 건 잘 모르겠으나 어

family lives, let alone to go on dates, since they had to work eight-hour shifts that were so laborious that they often ended up retiring early. What's more, even if they did have time to date doctors, it would most likely happen under pressure of authoritarianism, with the nurses subordinate to the doctors, rather than out of pure love. Concerning the other affair in the novel, it was said that it would be difficult for a feeling like love to sprout between a patient and nurse who was not only exposed to contagious and infectious germs from cleaning the patient's bloody pus and vomit, but also had to deal with the patient's dirty genitals when changing his urine tubes. In sum, nurses hammered at the point that the author relied on fantasy and romanticism rather than factual research. Finally, P.C.'s third novel was criticized as being too old-fashioned and didactic, since the two high-school students at the center of the story, which was narrated by their teacher, were depicted as tenacious yet also innocent—traits that adults considered representative of "good" kids.

It so happened that I owned all three books. The third one, in particular, had been praised as a typical story of hope and healing, at the time of its publication. I'd given several copies of it to moth-

디로도 치우치지 않고 일상에 널린 참괴와 환멸을 용의주도하게 피해가며 자신의 삶에 성공적으로 안착한 뒤 아이를 최소한 넷은 낳아 길러서 국가에 이바지하는 것 이외의 다른 가능성을 생각한 적 없어 보이는 사람이 쓰는 반듯한 세계관의 이야기를 굳이 읽을 필요가 있겠느냐는 동문서답으로 때워서 그들 가운데 적어도 세 명을 실망시키거나 혼란에 빠뜨렸고, 이때 서로 언성을 살짝 높인 두 사람의 사이가 싸늘해졌기에, 다음에는 실로 취향이 통하는 친구가 아닌 다음에야 선불리 책 선물 같은 것은 말아야겠다고 결심하기도 했었다.

어쨌거나 거론되는 사안들의 파편은 시간이 지남에 따라 타임라인에서 그대로 밀려날 듯하면서도 잊을 만하면 한두 번씩 되는 리트윗으로 고로롱팔십의 받은기침처럼 생명력을 획득했기에, 더 이상 두고만 볼 수는 없었는지 그사이 P씨와 협의를 마친 듯한 출판사가 메인 트윗에 자사 홈페이지 공지사항의 링크를 걸어놓았다. 그러나 그 공지는 안 그래도 미적지근했던 P씨의 대응에 이미 실망할 대로 실망한 독자들을 분노의 단계로 이동하도록 부채질했다.

ers who were invested in their children's education. We'd then met in a coffee shop, after a volunteer gig at the school our children attended. The moms' general opinions were typical and commonsensical —yet also contradictory: they were hopeful that their daughters and sons would grow up to be like the two main characters, yet also concerned with not wanting their children to stand out among their peers, like the two students in the book had, who became embroiled in troubles as they tried to help their teacher who tended to create problems. The moms hoped their own children would focus on schoolwork and college entrance exams. One of the moms voiced her opinion by saying she'd wondered how the children were able to make the right choices, resolving conflicts without losing confidence or wandering too far from their paths, when faced with the situations described in the book; and since she considered dynamism to be the main requisite for successful character descriptions in fiction, she believed that the author's view of the world was naïve and flat. Another mom chimed in that it seemed highly implausible and lazy on the writer's part to have the children go astray and then return to the right track only for the sake of the story, and, further, that the two inno-

본사에서 발간한 P작가의 신작 소설에 큰 관심을 보여주셔서 감사드립니다. 우선 P작가가 익명으로 활동하는 저자로서의 특색을 유지하기 위해 본인의 계정이 아닌 출판사가 대리 발표하는 점을 헤아려주시면 고맙겠습니다. 이 소설은 작가가 데뷔 당시부터 관심을 가지고 3년간의 자료 조사와 구성 끝에 완성한 것으로, 소설에 등장한 각종 사례와 인물 묘사는 조사 과정에서 만난 사람들의 일화와 배경을 변용하거나 자료에 기초한 순수 창작이며, 누구를 폄하하거나 공격할 의도로 씌어진 게 아닙니다. 다만 인물의 개성을 드러내고 사회의 이면을 풍자함에 있어서 과도한 묘사나 진술이 따랐을 수 있으며, 이는 대다수 작가들이 창작을 할 때 부딪히는 대상화의 문제를 P작가 역시 피해가지 못한 결과라고 볼 수 있습니다. 더구나 이 소설은 P작가가 처음으로 시도하는 사회물인 만큼 세계관 표출과 상황 전개에 있어 다소 정치하지 못했을 가능성도 있습니다. 이런 부족함을 앞으로 발전하는 과정의 하나로 여겨주시면 작가에게 그 이상의 격려는 없을 것이며, 이와 같은 설정이나 소재로 인해 누군가에게 상처가 되었다면 독자님들께 사과드립니다. 이 소설은 실존하는 타인의 명예를 작품 내에서 직접 훼손하거나 타인을 약취하는 등의 범죄행위와는 무관하므로 시중에서 책을 회수하는 조치는 없을 예정입니다. 또한 내

cent and pure children staying innocent and pure throughout the narrative was what was unique and interesting about the novel. Another mom remarked that there was no rule that the main characters in novels needed to get back on the right track, which prompted yet another comment: whether it would have been better to have the children stay ruined at the end of the story, and the other choice the writer could have made was to write about tainted children who stayed tainted; she also asserted that the novel told only half the story about children's education since the main characters were high-school students receiving a formal education, ignoring the education and care of students outside of school.

Then the moms turned to face me, since I had provided the book, and asked whose side I was on. I said I didn't have intelligent things to say about the book and gave them something of an incoherent answer: perhaps there was no need to read a story written by someone with a "prim and proper" worldview, who seemed to have carefully avoided shame and disillusionment in life without ever swaying one way or another, and who had successfully settled down, never thinking about other possibilities than serving the country by giving birth

부 논의 끝에, 재쇄 시 해당 부분들을 수정하거나 삭제하는 것 또한 작품의 전체 맥락과 구조를 해치게 되어 좋은 해결책이 아니라고 보았습니다. 이 부분 독자님들의 너른 이해를 구하며, 다음 작품에서 더욱 발전한 작가의 모습을 응원 및 기대해 주시기를 부탁드립니다.

도서출판 ○○ 편집부.

이 공지에 대한 최초의 반응은 그 똥 참 길게도 싸네, 였다. 결국 이것도 못하겠고 저것도 안 되겠으니 너네가 다 이해해라, 싫으면 보지 마라네? 독자를 무시하는 OO사의 책은 오늘부터 모두 불매합니다. 이를 시작으로 대규모 성토의 타래가 뒤를 이었다. 우선 '과도한' '다소' '가능성' '부족함' 등의 애매모호한 표현들로 때워서 자사 발간 도서의 문제점을 깨끗이 인정하기보다는 외부에서 핑곗거리를 찾는 느낌을 주며, '대다수의 문제'라는 말로 다른 멀쩡한 작가들 머리채를 잡아끄는 물귀신 작전에, 맥락도 못 찾는 사람들로 독자 수준을 후려치고 있다는 원성이 나왔다. 그중 독자로서의 목소리 이전에 도서를 구입한 행위에 초점을 맞춘, 즉 실속에 예민한 소비자들은 자기들이 스스로 인정할 정도로 '부

to and raising several children. My answer left several of them disappointed or confused, and the discussion caused two of the moms to raise their voices and ended up creating a rift between them. I' d decided never to give books to people other than friends who I knew shared my views.

Over time, the issues surrounding P.C.'s works seemed to disappear from Twitter, although they were retweeted once in a while, regaining life in spurts, like the dry coughing of an 80-year-old man. The publishers, perhaps thinking they could not sit and wait any longer for the controversy to die down, and seemingly after having reached an agreement with P.C., tweeted a link to a notice on their website. But this notice just added fuel to the smoldering fire, reigniting the anger of the readers, who were already as disappointed by P.C.'s non-response:

> We would like to thank our readers for their interest in the new book by writer P.C. that we have published. First, we ask for your understanding that we are making this announcement on behalf of P.C., as the author writes under a pseudonym. The latest book was something the author had been interested in since his literary debut, and was completed after three years of research and writing. The events and characters in the book are purely fictional,

족한' 소설을 출간하고 유료 판매한 출판사의 비양심적 상혼이야말로 모든 문제의 근원이라는 입장을 취했다. 앞으로 발전하는 과정으로 여겨달라니, 아무리 사소한 공산품이라도 각종 시험과 검수를 거친 합격품을 내놓는 법인데 돈 받고 파는 책이 미래를 위한 발판 수준의 시험작이라니, 독자를 봉 취급하는 데에도 정도가 있다는 것이었다.

한편 사태가 이 지경인데 본인은 한가롭게 사진이나 올리고 출판사에 대리 발표를 시키는 P씨의 인성 및 사고능력에 대한 진단이 이어졌다. 지금이 과연 익명 저자로서의 권리를 계속 찾아도 되는 상황인지에 대해 당사자 없는 공간에서의 난상토론 끝에, 익명의 정체성을 그대로 가져가더라도 최소한 이번만은 본인이 직접 등판해야 하는 일인데 큰 회사 뒤에 숨어 혼자 고고한 척하는 건 비열한 행위이며, 그토록 철저한 비밀주의 엄수를 구실로 댈 것 같으면 애당초 SNS 계정을 파지 말았어야 한다는 결론이 내려졌다. 계정조차 본인 것 아닌 팬이나 출판사가 돌리는 봇일지도 모른다는 가정에다가, 시원을 따지기 시작하면 계정은 둘째 치고 애당초 책 같은 것도 쓰지 않았어야 마땅한 거냐는 소수의

based on events and people the author encountered while conducting research, and were not created with any intention to belittle or attack particular individuals. However, some descriptions and statements made in order to express a character's individuality or to satirize the society we live in may have been excessive. This is the result of the fact that, like most writers, P.C. was unable to avoid the issue of objectification. As the first work of social fiction attempted by the author, it is also possible that the author was not politic enough in expressing a worldview or developing the storyline. If readers would graciously understand that these flaws are a few bumps along the author's path of growth as a writer nothing would be more encouraging to him. We humbly apologize to readers who might have been hurt by the events and characters portrayed in the novel. As the book does not directly defame any real-life individuals and the writer has not committed any criminal act, such as plagiarizing ideas, we have decided not to withdraw the book from the marketplace. In addition, through meetings and discussions, we have agreed that removing or editing parts of the book for re-publication would not be a good solution, as it would ruin the overall context and structure of the story. We ask for our readers' understanding concerning these decisions and their support for P.C.'s progress in future works.

XX Publishing

반문이 있었지만 말 그대로 소수였으며, 얼마 뒤엔 샐린저와 쥐스킨트를 비롯한 몇몇 사례가 언급되고, 최소한 그들은 얼굴과 이름이라도 깠지 그거랑 이거랑 같냐를 시작으로 비밀주의자와 전략적 은둔자의 개념이 뒤엉키는 한편, 어디 헬조선의 삼류 글쟁이를 외국의 거장들에게 갖다 대느냐는 준엄한 일갈이 사방에서 창궐했다.

나로 말할 것 같으면 그 수많은 타래에 멘션을 직접 섞지는 않았으며 약간 흥미를 갖고 지켜보는 정도였다. 무언가를—누군가를 표현하고 논평할 만큼의 말발과 글발이 달리는 문제도 있거니와, 아무 데라도 한두 마디나 혹은 전체 사안 중 극히 일부에 동조하는 말을 얹었다 치면 그것은 곧 가볍고 제한적이며 선별적 동의가 아닌 적극적 변호이자 독선적 '쉴드'이며 그 나머지를 배제하는 행위로 간주되어 불똥이 튀는 경우를 종종 보아왔으므로, 어느 흙탕물에도 발을 담그지 않으려면 입을 열지 않는 게 최선이라는 사실쯤 알고 있었다. 참전이 아닌 관전. 나는 철저한 관중으로서의 권리와 여흥을 누렸다. 짧은 글들의 맹사(猛射)가 나열되자 사람이 대체로 어디서 꼭지가 돌고 뚜껑이 열리는지 압력의 평

The first reaction to this notice was that it was a never-ending "shit parade." Comments appeared like: "Since we can't do this or that, readers should understand? If you don't want to read it, don't? Well, I'm boycotting all books from XX Publishing, which disrespects its readers." And this was just the beginning of the unraveling of a colossal denunciation of P.C. People claimed that by using ambiguous words such as "excessive," "not very," "possible," and "few bumps," the publisher was making excuses instead of acknowledging that the problem was with the book they had published; that they were dragging down other writers, who had no such problems, with the phrase "like most writers," and insulting readers as not being able to read between the lines. Among them, the readers who only focused on the nature of trade in their purchase of the book, in other words consumers who were sensitive to what they got for their money, took the stance that the publisher was the root of all the problems, since they had unleashed what they saw as a "flawed" book in an unscrupulous quest for money. These customers were outraged about being duped and treated like easy marks. "Support for the writer's progress in future works? Even the smallest, most trivial products are created

균값을 측정할 수 있었는데, 그러면서도 비등점은 제각각이라는 점이 특기할 만했다. 그리 오래지 않은 SNS 경험에 따르면 그곳의 말들은 전기포트 속 물방울이었다. 포르르 끓다가 부서지는 거품이 수면에 다시 합류했다. 일부는 증발하여 공기 중을 떠돌았다. 그대로 두자 물은 식었다. 때를 보아 스위치를 넣으면 다시 끓어 방울진 거품을 피워 올렸다. 그 과정을 무수히 반복하면 거품의 토대가 되는 수면의 높이만큼은 어느새 눈에 띄게 낮아진다는 사실이, 예정된 부서짐에도 불구하고 말을 그치거나 가두지 않는 이유일 터였다…… 그런 점에서 몇몇 부작용에도 불구하고 유의미한 난장이라는 인식 정도는 있었지만, 세상은 아무렴 주전자보다는 크고 넓을뿐더러, 그 유의미에 내가 뭔가를 보태기에는 에너지가 빈곤했다. 저마다 입에 칼을 물고 손에 도끼를 들었는데도 구체적인 형태가 없는 전기적 신호의 공간에서 최상의 포지션은 구경꾼이었다. 안 그래도 충분히 바쁜 일상을 영위하고 있었다. 아이들이 다니는 초중학교의 학부모회를 비롯한 각종 봉사는 작년부로 물러났지만, 때마침 친정과 시가에 질병과 빚보증과 철이 덜 든 남동생의 사업 실패 등 크고 작은 환난이 생겨 늘

through prototypes and tests, yet the publisher is insisting on having people pay for a book that is just a prototype for a better future product?"

In the meantime, people started analyzing P.C.'s character and critical thinking skills because "he" was posting pictures casually while the controversy was happening. After a long and frenzied discussion about whether or not it was reasonable for P.C. to insist on the right to anonymity at this point, people decided it was cowardly of him to hide behind the publisher and to act high and mighty when he should at least make a personal apology, even while maintaining his anonymity. They concluded that it would be better for the author not to have a Twitter account at all if he wanted to stay absolutely anonymous. Some speculated that his social media account might not even be real, but a Twitterbot created by the publisher or a fan, while a few argued that P.C. shouldn't even have written books, let alone created a social media account; but these more extreme opinions were voiced by only a few. Then, a few days later, someone mentioned the reclusive American writer J.D. Salinger and German recluse-author Patrick Süskind, which once again spurred a flurry of retorts: "At least they

신경이 곤두선 상태에서, 책을 읽는다든지 사람들의 반응을 눈여겨본다든지 하는 일도 일종의 사치였다. 육체적 실무와 감정노동을 제외하더라도, 누구도 증오하지 않으며 어디에도 환멸을 느끼지 않는 것처럼 보이는 삶을 꾸리는 일이란, 생각보다 높은 칼로리의 에너지를 필요로 했다. 친밀한 사람들—그보다는 서로 조심해야 할 관계로 이루어진 그물망을 유지 보수하기 위해 단순성과 모호성을 동시에 장착하고 자유로이 구사해야 했다. 삶이 오엑스 퀴즈와 같다면 그 중간에 발을 걸치고 서 있다가, 어느 쪽으로든 건너오라는 요구를 받으면 다수가 선 자리로 이동하는 식이었다. 반드시 누군가를 만족시키기 위한 제스처라기보다는, 그것이 내가 생각하는 최선이자 최소한의 올바름이었다.

유수 종합 출판사가 P씨의 책만 출간한 것도 아닌 데다 당장 그의 책이 수십만 부 베스트셀러라도 되어서 특별 관리 보호 작가로 돌보는 상황도 아닌 모양, 지속적 피드백에 신경 쓰지 못하고 마침내 총알받이로서의 기능을 상실한 이틀 뒤, P씨가 자신의 계정에 다음과 같은 간단명료한 글을 올렸다.

didn't hide behind anonymity, so it isn't the same," and prompting discussions in which the concepts of the secretive figure and the strategic hermit became entangled, leading to heated attacks against those who mentioned Salinger and Süskind for comparing a third-rate writer from "Hell Joseon" to great authors from abroad.

As for me, I didn't comment in any of these threads, instead observing with curiosity from afar. I wasn't eloquent or articulate enough to critique or discuss something or someone, and I'd occasionally seen how people who added in a word of agreement on a small matter would become victims of a backlash, harshly accused of advocating or self-righteously shielding the person or thing under criticism, when all they had done was offer an innocent agreement with some limited information. I knew it was best not to partake in this kind of controversy if I were to avoid stepping in dirty mud puddles.

Observing, rather than taking part in these discussions, I enjoyed my stance as a member of the audience: sitting back, observing, and being entertained. A fusillade of brief comments provided me with a means of deducing general points that ticked off people and or made them fly off the handle, and it was also interesting to see how ev-

저는 다큐가 아닌 소설을 썼을 뿐입니다. 소설로 누군가를 다치게 할 생각은 지금도 앞으로도 없습니다. 그럼에도 본의 아니게 어떤 개인이나 집단이 불편을 느끼셨다면 죄송합니다.

P씨는 여전히 얼굴과 실명 등 정체를 까지 않았으나, 적어도 캡션 없는 사진이나 다른 책 인용구를 제외하고 거의 처음으로 들려주다시피 하는 본인의 목소리이자, 140자라는 글자 수 한계상 최소한의 이유와 구실을 배제하고 단순 입장과 소회만 밝힌 글이었다. 그러자 이번에는 최초의 반응이, 너무 성의 없이 자기 하고 싶은 말만 툭 던지고 사라진다—였다. 출판사는 해명을 하랬더니 변명을 하고 앉았는가 하면 P씨는 변명이란 없는 대신 설명도 대안도 없으니 총체적 난국이라 했다. 죄송하다는 한마디는 사뭇 귀찮다는 뉘앙스로 이제 해달라는 대로 해줬으니 그만 떠들라는 말의 다른 표현으로 보이며, 더욱이 '느끼셨다면'이라는 조건을 붙인 것은 실제로 상처 입은 사람들을 지우는 동시에, 귀에 걸면 귀걸이 코에 걸면 코걸이가 되는 '불편'이라는 말을 선택함으로써 자신의 책임을 인정하지 않는 태도라 했다. 그러므로 그의 붓끝이 놀린 말 가운데 정확히 무엇이

eryone had a different anger threshold. According to my not-very-extensive experience with social media, the words people spewed out were like drops of water in an electric kettle: bubbles formed, crashed at the surface, and them merged with the water again, although some of it evaporated and remained in the air. When left on its own, though, the kettle simmered down. But when the electricity was turned on again, the water boiled and bubbled to the surface all over again. After countless repetitions of boiling and simmering down, the level of the water fell significantly, which was probably why some people did not kept their thoughts to themselves or stop talking, despite the bubbling and crashing at the surface. In fact, I was aware that these chaotic discussions could be meaningful despite a few side-effects. But the world was definitely bigger than a kettle, and I did not have enough energy to add something to it. Everyone had knives clenched in their teeth and axes in their hands, in a space created by electric signals instead of physical space, so it seemed wisest to stay on the side lines.

In any case, I was busy with my own life. I'd stopped volunteering and had withdrawn from the PTAs in my children's elementary and middle

잘못되었으며 그가 어떤 오류를 저질렀는지, 무엇보다 이후 어떤 수정 조치가 따를 것인지를 명시하는 2차 해명서가 필요하다는 지적이 따랐다. 이어서 폭주하는 멘션에 P씨는 답을 달지 않았으나 그렇다고 자신의 계정에 자물쇠를 채우지도 않았다.

—그래서 절필은 언제 하실 건데요?

—'앞으로도' 없다는 걸 보니 그러고도 계속 쓰긴 할 건가 보네.

—어쨌거나 깔린 책은 회수 안 하시겠다는 거죠?

—최소한 이미 팔린 책에 대해서는 토해내시는 게 맞죠. 도의적 책임이라도 느끼신다면 말이지만.

—그동안 자랑질했던 카메라들도 인세니 계약금이니 받아 샀을 텐데. 다 팔고 기부라도 해야 하지 않나.

그러자 다음 날엔 2차 해명 대신 좀더 구체적인 감정을 담은 글이 올라왔다.

설정상 그렇게밖에 쓸 수 없는 부분이 있습니다. 내용 진행을 위해서입니다. 양해 부탁드립니다. 직업이나 처지나 성별을 바꿔볼까 하는 생각도 없지 않았습니다. 그러나 어떻게 해봐도 느낌이 살지 않아서 원래 생각대로 썼습니다.

schools; but illnesses in both my and my husband's families, a younger brother's failed business, and other problems at home, both big and small, put me constantly on edge; so reading books and even watching people's reactions to them was a luxury. Even excluding the physical activity and emotional labor I had to perform, more energy and calories were needed to lead a life of pretending to hate no one and despising nothing. In order to constantly repair and maintain a network of close acquaintances—a group of people with whom I needed to keep a close but not-too-close distance, far but not-too-far—I had to equip myself with both simplicity and ambiguity and to employ them at will. It was like living a life like an "Yes/No" quiz, in which I had to tow the middle way and go with the majority if called on. It wasn't necessarily a gesture to satisfy someone, but rather what I deemed, at the least, the best and most righteous decision.

The publisher didn't publish only P.C.'s books, of course, and it wasn't as though P.C. was a best-selling author with works that sold millions of copies, and so an author who required special management and protection. So, finally, two days after the publisher failed to respond to the continuous feedback from readers and kept protecting P.C.

첫 번째 트윗이 30여 회 리트윗되는 동안 P씨는 두 번째 연결 트윗을 올렸다.

> 서로 다른 입장들을 고려하고 지나치게 균형을 맞추려다 전체의 그림이 어그러지는 것보다는, 누군가가 조금 불편하더라도 소설의 개연성과 완성도에 집중하는 게 맞다고 보았습니다. 현실에 아주 없는 일을 쓴 것도 아니고 소설적 과장과 허구가 들어간 겁니다.

그의 육성이 조금 더 추가되자 빠른 속도로 반응이 달렸다. 한 시간 만에 200여 회의 리트윗이 되고 타래는 이러했다.

—느낌 안 산다는 것도 자기 생각일 뿐. 어떻게 해도 느낌이 안 산다면 능력 부족의 증거.

—타인을 배려하고 균형을 맞추는 행위가 지나친 일이라는 분, 잘 가세요. 멀리 안 나가요.

—양념 반 후라이드 반도 아니고 언제 균형 맞춰달랬나요? 머리를 쓰고 공부를 하랬지. 누군가를 꼭 불편하게 만들고 싶으면 님이나 님 가족을 제물로 삼지, 왜 애매한 사람들을 갖고 그러는지.

from the line of fire, P.C. posted two tweets:

> I only write fiction; they are not non-fiction. I do not wish to hurt people with my works now or in the future.
>
> Nevertheless I apologize if certain groups or individuals were made uncomfortable.

While P.C. continued to maintain anonymity, these were the first-ever messages from him aside from caption-less photos and sentences taken from other books: a simple expression of a position and an opinion given without an excuse, taking into account the 140-character constraints. People's first reaction was: "P.C. has tossed us an insincere apology and disappeared again." It was a complete mess: the publisher had made excuses instead of providing an explanation, and P.C. had neither made an excuse nor offered an explanation or a solution to the problem. People said that the writer's apology was laced with annoyance, as though saying, "I've done what you wanted me to do, so stop talking about it," and argued that the conditional "if" had negated those who were genuinely hurt by his book, while at the same time, by using "uncomfortable," which could be interpreted any way one wanted, P.C. was not taking full responsibility for

—설정상 그렇게밖에 안 된다면 애당초 설정부터 바꿨으면 되는 문제잖아요? 출판사나 님이나 지금 계속 전체 그림 무너진다고 징징대는데, 그렇게 무너질 그림이면 처음부터 그리지를 말라고.

—그놈의 소설적 과장과 허구는 왜 만날 약자만을 대상으로 하는지 모를…….

—그런 구린 방법을 써야만 내용 진행을 할 수 있다는 것 자체가 이미 자기가 얼마나 게으른지를 광고하는 거 아닌가…… 지금껏 버셨으면 이제 그만 하심이.

—됐고, 그래서 지금 님한테는 이 개연성이랑 완성도가 만족스러운가 보죠? 거기에 집중하느라 다른 걸 내다 버리셨다니까. 그것만 한번 말씀해보세요.

P씨가 입을 열수록 사태는 진정되기는커녕 게 자루를 풀어놓은 듯했다. 전체 타래 가운데 비웃음이 약 50퍼센트로 제일 높은 비중을 차지했으며 30퍼센트가 맹비난이었다. 20퍼센트는 『가르강튀아 · 팡타그뤼엘』이나 『인생의 첫출발』 같은 목록을 예로 들며 예로부터 풍자적 묘사란 기괴한 이방의 존재들, 신체가 뒤틀리거나 왜곡된 사람들, 어딘가 모자란 사람들이나 부스럼쟁이 등을 대상으로 이루어져온 만큼, 현대의 작가가 장애인

the controversy caused by his novel. As a result, people followed up those tweets with demands for a second explanation from the writer that would explicitly state the problems with the novel, the errors committed, and the kind of revisions planned for the future. But P.C. didn't comment on the explosion of comments. And he didn't close his social media account.

—So when are you going to stop writing?

—Since you said "in the future," I guess that means you'll keep on writing?

—Anyway, you're saying that you're not going to take the books back?

—You should at least cough up the money you got for the books that were sold, if you have any conscience.

—(1/2) Didn't you buy all the cameras you'd bragged about with royalties and payments from your books?

—(2/2) Shouldn't you sell them and at the very least donate the money?

The next day, P.C. posted several more emotional tweets, although it wasn't a full explanation:

이나 외국인을 오락적 소재로 삼았다고 하여 비난하는 것은 폭력적 염결주의라는 주장을 펴기도 했으나, 이는 P씨를 얘기하는데 본질을 벗어나서 이국의 라블레와 발자크를 끌어오느라 먹물들이 퍽이나 애쓴다는 조롱과 함께 묻혔다. 그사이 시일이 두 달 남짓 흘렀으므로 P씨의 신작은 자연스레 종합순위에서 자취를 감췄고, 그 뒤로 미디어 판권이 계약되었다는 소식은 들려오지 않았다. 그리하여 책이 폭발적인 반응을 얻을 기회를 잃었으므로, 대부분의 사람들 기억에서도 밀려났다. 매일 새로운 사건이, 주로 사고가 있었으며 그전의 사건은 너무 익어 발끝에 떨어진 무른 열매 같았다. 이미 출판사는 자사의 다른 신간 홍보에 집중하느라 아무 일도 없었다는 듯 각종 실용서와 교양인문서를 소개하는 중이었고, 실상 그런 책들이 더 많이 화제도 되고 팔려나갔으므로, P씨의 거취에 대해 출판사 계정에 문의하는 글은 곧 뜸해졌다. P씨의 계정에는 다시 일상적인 사진이 가끔가다 올라오기 시작했으며 사람들은 분위기 있게 찍힌 사진을 관성적으로 리트윗만 할 뿐 더 이상 그의 지나간 책에 대해 캐지 않았다. 그것을 힐문할 만큼의 관심과 여력이 있는 사람들은 이미 그 타래를 떠나

Please understand that for the sake of the story there were parts that I couldn't change. It was necessary for the progress of the narrative.

While this first tweet was retweeted immediately about 30 times, P.C. posted the following tweets:

I thought about changing the character's situations, sexes, and jobs, but no matter how hard I tried, I couldn't make it work. So I decided to keep what I had.

I believed it best to focus on making a story plausible and effective, even if it might make some people uncomfortable,

rather than ruining the big picture by weighing everyone's feelings and going to extremes to present balanced opinions.

I only added some literary exaggeration and imagination to what could happen in reality.

With this bit of P.C.'s voice added to the controversy, replies and comments followed rapidly. The writer's postings were retweeted over 200 times within an hour, with comments such as:

가 다른 주제에 집중하느라 P씨와 그의 사생활이 눈에 들어오지 않았다. 적어도 그가 새 책을 내놓음으로써 사정거리 안으로 재진입하기 전까지는.

그다음 해에 출간된 P씨의 다섯 번째 전작 장편소설은, 지난번 논란을 의식한 결과인지 상대적으로 안전한 수비 범위 안에서 인물들이 움직이고 있었다. 그가 겪어내고 직접 부대끼며 살았을 가능성이 높은, 그러므로 현장감 좋고 굴절률이 작은 묘사를 기대할 수 있는 일상생활 테마의 가족극이기도 했거니와, 문제적 인물이나 상황이 줄었으며, 큰 굴곡 없이 평탄하다 가끔 완만한 곡선을 그린 뒤 제자리로 안착하는 갈등 구조를 지녔다. 그러고 보니 P씨는 이미 그전에도 불륜 묘사에서 증명한바, 다른 쪽의 역량은 몰라도 으레 중대히 다뤄질 법한 상황과 사건에 대해 호들갑을 떨지 않는 잔잔한 터치 감각 정도는 있었다. 샘물과 바람과 나뭇잎과 다람쥐 정도만 존재하는 듯싶은 세계를 그려내는 것도 재능이었다. 그러나 이렇다 할 만한 사건이 발생하지 않는 서사를 한 권 분량으로 흥미를 유지한 채 이끌고 나갈 엄두는 처음부터 내지 못한 듯, 인물들이 한 번씩 폴리스 라인을 넘을 뻔했다가 돌아오는 고전적 패턴이

—Couldn't make it work? Well, if no matter how you try you can't get it to work—that means you suck.

—So considering people's feelings and presenting balanced opinions are too much? Bye-bye, never see you again.

—(1/2) What the heck: did we ever ask you for balanced opinions? Use your head and do more research.

—(2/2) If you wanted to make someone uncomfortable, you could've just written about you or your family instead of all those other people.

—(1/2) For the sake of the story? Then you should've changed the story. Both you and the publisher are complaining...

—(2/2) about ruining the big picture—but maybe you should stop painting the picture if it's not gonna work.

—Always excuses about literary exaggeration and imagination only when portraying socially vulnerable people.

—Well, doesn't using such disgusting means to make a story work show that the author's lazy to begin with? Maybe stop writing.

—So, you're fine with the story, you mean? Seems like you got everything else wrong, so now

엿보이기도 했다. 오래 앓던 시모의 장례가 끝난 뒤 아내가 남편의 휴대전화에 문자메시지 한 통만 남긴 채 트렁크를 끌고 가출하는 것이 이야기의 시작이었다. 바로 그녀가 중심 화자가 되었으므로, 사람들은 그전에 내내 작가 자신의 페르소나로 추정되는 30대 중반의 남자들만 전면에 내세웠던 P씨가 조금은 달라지려 노력했다는 점을 눈치챌 수 있었다. 한편 그녀의 고교생 딸은 학교를 일찌감치 떠난 친구를 우연히 만났다가 일행의 꼬드김에 빠져 30대 중반의 회사원과 조건만남을…… 가졌다면 또다시 큰 파장을 일으켰겠지만, 사태는 그쪽으로 흘러가지 않았다. 약속 장소에 나타난 회사원은 아빠의 부하직원이었던 것이다.

몇 가지 아슬아슬한 지점을 돌파하면서 용케도 휘청거리지 않은 이야기에 대해, P씨의 애독자들은 그전과 달라진 점이나 나아졌다고 판단하는 점을 꼽아 자기 블로그나 SNS에 올려놓았는데, 그중에는 몇몇 키워드 노출로 출판사의 의뢰를 받고 쓴 티가 심하게 나는 바이럴마케터들도 있었다. 작년에 있던 소란의 주인공 정도로 P씨를 기억하는 새로운 독자들은 호기심에 넘겨보았다가, 역시 사람들이 말리는 콘텐츠는 건드리는 게

let's talk about that.

The more P.C. communicated, the worse it became, rather than calming down. About half of all the replies to P.C.'s tweets were sneers, and almost one-third were scathing attacks; the remaining were supportive, mentioning works such as *The Life of Gargangtua and Pantagruel* or *Un debut dans la vie*, and arguing that satirical descriptions have always been used to portray eccentric strangers, people with disabilities, physical distortions, mental disabilities, and the like, and therefore criticizing a contemporary writer for using the same techniques for the purpose of entertaining readers was a violent manifestation of prudish political correctness. But those positive comments were buried under the derision; people scoffed at and mocked those who mentioned Rabelais and Balzac for trying to sound smarter by citing foreign writers, when they should be focusing on P.C.

By that time, about two months had passed since the publication of the novel, and it fell off the bestseller list. Also, there were no longer any rumors about film producers wanting to purchase the media rights. Since the book had missed garnering a tremendously successful reception, it slipped quiet-

아니라며 넌더리를 내곤 떨어져나갔다. 이번에 문제가 된 대목은 이러했다. 주인공 여성이 병든 시모를 쭉 모셨다는 대목부터가 고릿적 시절의 티브이 주말 대가족극에서 무한 반복 및 소비되는 맏며느리 이미지를 벗지 못했으며, 트렁크를 끌고 나선 정도가 무슨 대단한 일탈인 양 묘사되는 데 헛웃음이 나온다는 이야기였다. 그 와중에 그녀는 현관을 나서기 전 다섯 시간에 걸쳐 집안 대청소와 식구들 빨래를 마치고 그걸 건조대에 하나하나 널어놓기까지 했다는 것. 특히 압권이었던 건, 상하지만 않는다면 남편과 아들딸이 열흘은 두고 먹을 수 있는 밑반찬을 대량 제조한 뒤 종류별로 투명한 밀폐용기에 나눠 담아 라벨까지 붙여놓고 냉장고 칸칸이 쟁여두었다는 점이었다. 누군가는 그 정밀 묘사에서 한국 사회가 엄마에게 답습하기를 요구하는 모습의 전형이 느껴져 소름이 돋는 바람에 그대로 책을 도서관에 반납했다는 후기를 남겼다—마침 작성자 자신의 엄마 또한 수술을 앞두고 식구들 한 달 치 반찬부터 걱정하던 모습이 오버랩되었다는 첨언과 함께.

한편 남편과 아들에 대해서는 별다른 얘기가 없는데 왜 딸만 일탈 직전까지 가느냐 그것도 하필이면 엄마가

ly out of most people's memories. After all, every day some new big event, like an horrendous accident, occurred, and the "old" news would be discarded, like overripe fruit fallen at people's feet. As though nothing had happened, the publisher was busy promoting its latest how-to and nonfiction books; and since these were more popular and sold more copies, fewer and fewer people posted comments and inquiries on the publisher's social media account about P.C. Once again, pictures of daily life began to appear on the writer's Twitter account, and people retweeted them out of habit, no longer digging deeper and criticizing P.C. Those individuals who had had the interest and energy to keep criticizing him had left the thread to concentrate on something else and no longer cared about the writer and his life—until P.C. published a new book.

P.C.'s fifth full-length novel came out the next year. Perhaps because of the controversy the last book had caused, the characters in this latest work acted within relatively safe and defensible limits. The narrative was a family drama, one that it seemed highly likely the author had actually experienced, and therefore it had a vivid sense of reality and straight-forward descriptions. The novel contained few problematic characters and situations,

부재중일 때, 그건 여성이 위기 상황에서 상대적으로 나약하다고 부각하려는 의도이며, 엄마가 자리를 비운 책임이 그만큼 위중함을 강조하고자 조건만남 소재를 넣었다는 분석이 있었다. 더구나 만남의 상대가 하필 아빠와 같은 회사 직원이라는 우연의 타당성은 차치하고라도, 회사원은 상사의 딸이라는 걸 알지 못했는데도—딸이 남자의 정체를 알아본 이유는 아빠의 야유회 단체사진에서 본 얼굴이기 때문—그녀가 18세라는 걸 알자 근사한 저녁과 옷만 사주고 잘 달래서 돌려보냈다는 점이 수목 멜로드라마에서나 볼 수 있는 판타지라는 지적도 나왔다. 친구의 함정에 빠진 여학생이 순전히 남자 어른의 변심과 동정에 기대어 그 상황을 모면한다는 것으로, 문제 해결을 남자가 하도록 하여 여학생을 수동적 존재로 묘사하고, 그런 품위 있는 남자란 적어도 이 땅에는 존재하지 않으며, 남성들 일반에 씌워진 혐의를 벗겨보고자 몸부림치는 작가의 작위가 느껴지는데, 그래봤자 애당초 조건만남에 응하여 그 자리에 나온 것부터가 이미 틀려먹은 인간이라는 점에서 인물 묘사의 일관성마저 떨어진다는 것이었다. 결국 P씨는 이번에 큰맘 먹고 엄마와 딸을 중심으로 한 이야기를 써

and its conflict had a gradual arc, without too much fluctuation, landing within the range of the socially acceptable. Come to think of it, P.C.'s previous writings had always had a sense of subtlety and restraint, if nothing else—they didn't make a fuss about something that could have been treated importantly, as in the portrayal of some affairs in a previous book. Certainly, it would take some skill to depict a fairytale world in which it was always spring, populated only by the wind, dancing leaves, and chipmunks. But P.C. probably couldn't write a whole book that didn't have a major conflict or event, so this latest novel did have a classical pattern of characters and events pushed to the edge, just not crossing the line.

The story opened with a woman leaving home with a suitcase. She did so after texting her husband following the funeral of her mother-in-law, who had suffered for years from an illness. Since the woman was the main narrator, people could appreciate that P.C. had attempted to change his usual line-up of men in their 30s, which P.C. himself was assumed to inhabit. The daughter of the protagonist was a high-school student, who runs into a friend who'd dropped out of school, and who is goaded into engaging in "compensated dating." If

보고자 했겠으나 실은 자신이 그것을 시도했다는 사실 자체에 취했을 뿐, 사유 부족 또는 공부 부족으로 그전과 달라진 점은 없다는 종합 결론이 내려졌다. 그럼에도 소설의 절정과 결말은 비교적 순하게 흘러간 데다 화제성과 판매 지수 또한 전 같지 않아서 예년과 달리 출판사의 계정으로 민원이 폭주하지는 않았고 다만 '당신이 집에서 부인을 어떤 존재로 취급하는지 잘 알겠다' 내지는 '솔직히 말해봐요 조건만남 해봤죠? 여고생이 나오는 바람에 철창 갈까 겁나서 용돈만 쥐여주고 보내셨다거나?' 정도의 비소가 한두 달에 걸쳐 간간이 달렸다. 적어도 입장 표명이나 해명 요구의 움직임이 있던 전년도보다는 나았지만 나는 이번에도 P씨의 책을 장바구니 대신 기약 없는 보관함으로 옮기고, 누구에게든 선물할 생각을 접어두었다. 도대체가 이 시대에 책 선물이라니 어림 반 푼어치 없는 이야기이기도 하고, 세상 읽고 볼 것들 천지인데 원래 책이란 꼭 필요한 것만 도서관에서 빌려 읽으면 된다고 보통들 여기니까. 신간에 대한 일반의 관심과 조소가 사라질 무렵, P씨는 그전의 누적된 멘션들에 대한 일종의 답을—이제 와선 누구도 새삼 확인하러 들어오지 않을 한마디를 올려놓고 또

this "dating" had actually happened, it would've led to another controversy, but that wasn't how the story progressed: the man who showed up at their meeting place was her father's subordinate.

About the story, which contained a few "close calls," but no calamities, P.C.'s fans wrote on their blogs and social media sites about what they saw as having changed or improved in P.C.'s book. Some of the observations were obviously written by viral marketers, though, using enticing keywords paid for by the publisher. New readers who merely remembered P.C. as the writer at the center of a controversy in the previous year grabbed the new book with curiosity, and then came away disgusted, saying: There was a reason you shouldn't do things others warned you about. This time, again, people found the main character to be problematic, citing a woman who had to take care of her ill mother-in-law as the trite and overused characterization of an eldest daughter-in-law so often featured in Korean family dramas. They also found it laughable that leaving home with a suitcase was described as a great breaking away. On top of that, before she leaves home, the mother and wife spends five hours cleaning the house, doing laundry, and hanging the clothes to dry on a rack. But

다시 SNS 휴식기를 가졌다.

현실에서만큼은 누구에게도 피해를 주지 않고 올바르게 살아가려고 노력 중이며 무엇보다도 저한테는 아내가 없습니다.

그간의 글 모두를 털어 비로소 밝힌 P씨의 유일한 개인 정보였다. 아내 없음.

이 글은 다음과 같은 세 개의 반응만 달린 채 타임라인 바깥으로 밀려났다.

—현실에서만큼은, 이라면 소설에서 누군가에게 피해를 줬다는 사실은 인정한다는 뜻인가요?

—소설을 읽고 상처받은 사람들은 현실에 존재하는 사람이 아닌가 보네.

—와, 사람들 다 잊어버릴 때까지 기다렸다가 한 줄씩 날리고 튀는 용의주도함 봐라. 안 물어봤어요, 안 궁금해요, 안 사요.

그리하여 이제 P씨의 가장 최근, 그리고 어쩌면 마지막 책에 대해서 이야기해야 할 것 같다. 그는 두 달 전, 지치지도 않고 반성도 없이 꾸준히 잘도 쏟아낸다는 눈

the "worst" part was that she made ten days' worth of side and main dishes for her husband, daughter, and son, putting them in clear, labeled containers, and stacking them neatly in the refrigerator. One reader left a review saying she had to return the book to the library right away because that part gave her goose bumps, as it reminded her of the image of selfless mothers the Korean society that had been forced on women, along with another comment about how the protagonist overlapped with her own mother, who had worried about what her family would have to eat for a month when she had to undergo an operation.

Others pointed out that, while there wasn't much about the husband and son, the daughter nearly commits a crime in her mother's absence, and analyzed how this was intended to show that women were relatively weak in crises, and the issue of compensated dating was included to emphasize how critical a mother's absence was to her children. Moreover, aside from the validity of the coincidence in which the man whom the daughter met was her father's subordinate, people criticized the section about the man buying her dinner and clothes and sending her home after finding out that she was only 18, without realizing she was his boss's daugh-

총을 받으며 신작 장편소설을 출간했는데, 여느 때보다 볼륨이 좀 작았다. 판형이며 표지 일러스트까지 어른을 위한 동화라는 느낌을 물씬 풍겨서, 이번에야말로 선물용이니 업어가라는 팬시한 오라를 서점 매장 진열대에서 뿜어내고 있었다. 내용과 설정은 그전보다도 한층 더 위험 요소—욕동(欲動)이든 열광이든 폭력이든, 하여간 식물적이지 않은 것들 가운데 위험하지 않은 게 있기나 한지 모르겠으나—가 빠져 있어서, 그런 P씨의 노력은 오래전 LP시대 국내 가수들의 앨범에 사이드A와 B의 마지막 트랙으로 꼭 한 곡씩 수록되어 있던 「어허야 둥기둥기」를 비롯한 건전가요 목록을 떠올리게 했다. 아무리 그래도 그렇지 개과천선한 문제아들의 농구대회 출전 우승기라니, 대놓고 감동팔이를 노린 듯한 클리셰에 좀 너무 내려놓고 쉽게 간다는 생각도 들었고, 그 푸르른 스토리와 인물들은 그가 더 이상 어떤 새로운 시도나 현실 반영 내지는 현실 변용을 하려는 의욕이 없다는 증거로 보였다. 그러나 그런 걸 필요로 하는 이들이 생각보다 많으니 이렇게 옷을 입고 나왔지, 어쨌거나 태어났다는 이유만으로 조난자가 된 사람들은 그런 맑은 서사를 구호물자처럼 여기기도 하며, 이

ter (the daughter had recognized him from a picture of a company picnic). People claimed that such generous behavior was the kind of fantasy usually reserved for evening soap operas. Some people argued that by having a high-school student avoid such a bad situation through the sympathy and change of heart of an adult male, the book was portraying girls as passive and men as dynamic and problem solvers. Moreover, people said, this kind of a decent man does not really exist, at least not on this planet. People opined that through the novel the author seemed bent on clearing men of such charges, while the fact that the man had come to meet a girl for sex was evidence of his pathetic state, and therefore his change was not even consistent with his character. In the end, these commenters concluded that P.C. had attempted, for a change, to write a story about a mother and daughter, but that it seemed the author was satisfied solely with making the attempt, and that nothing else had changed from previous works, either because of a lack of reflection or research. Nevertheless, the climax and ending of the novel were relatively moderate, and since the book's popularity and sales were not as high as P.C.'s previous books, there were fewer complaints to the publisher and only occasional

야기책 속에서마저 비애나 고난을 목도하기 원치 않는다 하니. 일부 고정 독자들은 냉소 가운데의 예기치 못한 폭소, 고소(苦笑) 가운데의 은근한 미소가 주력상품이었던 P씨가 차포 다 떼고 뭐하자는 건지 모르겠다는 의구심과 실망 섞인 의견을 내놓았다. 잔잔한 것도 좋지만 정도껏, 이전에 그의 잔잔함에는 그래도 간과하지 못할 긴장감이 있었는데, 지금은 밋밋하고 굴곡 없고 좋은 게 좋다는 식이고 더 이상 볼 필요가 없겠네요 하차합니다. 정말로 이제는 그만 써도 될 것 같아요…… 그런데 사람들은 생각보다 날카로운 면도날들을 저마다 혀 밑에 숨기거나 손끝에 꽂고 있어서, 종합순위 근처에도 가지 못한 이 농구 이야기 역시 서사의 포가 떠지는 걸 피해갈 수 없었다. 다섯 명의 선수들은 모두 소년원 출신으로 각각 폭행 상해 및 금품 갈취는 기본이며 그중엔 강간 미수마저 있는데, 그들로 인해 오랫동안 고통받은 사람들은 조명되지 않을뿐더러 이름조차 등장하지 않은 채 그 존재가 페이지 밖으로 지워지고, 어째서 선량한 이들을 괴롭힌 범죄자들은 운동하는 동안 눈물 콧물 짜내는 시늉 좀 하다가 승리를 거머쥐는가, 그들에게 우승컵을 들고 환호를 올릴 자격이 있나,

negative comments posted, such as "I can see how now you must treat your own wife at home." or "Be honest, you dated someone for money, right? And you found out she was a minor so you gave her money and sent her home because you were terrified of going to jail, right?" The situation wasn't as bad as the previous year, when people had demanded an explanation and apology from P.C., yet still I removed P.C.'s books from my shopping cart and saved them, before deciding not to buy them. Anyway, giving books as presents nowadays seemed quite ridiculous, since in a culture full of material to read and watch, people just take a book out of the library. Around the time when people's interest in and mockery of P.C.'s latest work began to subside, the author posted a reply to the feedback—although at that time, no one seemed interested in visiting his account—and then once again the writer went on a long hiatus from posting on social media:

> At least in reality, I am doing my best to lead a moral life and not hurt people, and, most importantly, I do not have a wife.

Among everything P.C. had written, that was the

그들은 자기들끼리는 반성회라고 가지면서 피해자들을 찾아다니며 사과한 적 있나. 소년원에서 단체생활을 한 것 말고는 이렇다 할 대가를 치르지 않은 자들이 감동의 주역이 된다니 모순이지 않나. P씨는 어둠에 웅크린 아이들을 끄집어낸다면서 그들로 인해 더욱 깊은 어둠 속에서 신음하는 이들의 목소리는 들려주지 않았고, 각각의 아이들에게 주정뱅이 아비와 병든 어미 내지는 집 나간 어미를 비롯한 식상한 배경을 끼얹음으로써 그들은 비행을 저지를 수밖에 없는 환경이었다는 손쉬운 면죄부를 주고 싶었던 게 아닐까(이때 집을 나가는 사람이 꼭 어미라는 점에서 여성을 무책임한 존재로 묘사하는 작가의 의도는 더 부연할 가치가 없겠다). 양쪽의 고통을 나태한 붓으로 팔아먹는 이야기를 예쁜 그림 좀 얹어다 책으로 엮어내고 재미 좀 보겠다는 출판사는, 언제까지 그런 식의 장사를 계속할 텐가.

안 그래도 사진이 올라오는 간격마저 뜸해졌던 P씨의 계정은 그즈음 마침내 자물쇠가 채워졌고, 5만여 명의 팔로워 가운데 이제 실제로 그를 지켜보는 소위 살아 있는 계정은 내 것을 비롯해 5천 명이나 될까 싶었는데, 서점 매대에서 책이 내려가고 얼마 뒤 그의 계정

only personal information the author had ever shared: no wife.

This tweet earned the following three replies, before it was pushed out of people's timelines and vanished into oblivion:

—"At least in reality?" Then you do acknowledge that you've hurt people through your novels?

—So then people who were hurt by your novels are not "real" people?

—Wow, waiting until everyone forgets, then writing an excuse and running off! Didn't ask, don't care, and won't be buying your books!

And now I want to talk about P.C.'s last book. Two months ago, the writer published another full-length novel—and the online community glower and scowl at him again for continuing to release new books without reflecting on past mistakes. The book was shorter than previous ones. From its format to its cover illustration, it was designed to look like a fairytale for adults. Multiple copies were featured on display tables in bookstores, with an aura of asking to be bought as gifts. There was much less risky material in it than his previous novels. Actually, I'm

은 삭제되었다. 그러나 마지막으로 보여준 이야기의 임팩트가 그리 크지 않았으므로 그가 사라진 것을 알아차리거나 그걸 두고 비아냥거리는 이들은 많지 않았다. 그들 중 누구도 출판사 계정에 문의를 넣지 않았고, 출판사가 P씨의 근황을 펠 만큼 그에게 공을 들이는 것처럼 보이지도 않았으나, 어쩐지 P씨는 소설가로서의 삶을 종료하고 자신의 일상이나 취미에 조용히 스며들었으리라는 확신이, 드는 것이었다. 그는 어떻게 해봐도 부족한 말들의 숲을 어설피 배회하는 자가 될 것이며, 어디서도 그의 발자국을 다시 발견하지는 못하리라는, 확신이.

문자메시지가 연달아 네 개 도착한 걸 확인하느라 인터넷 창을 닫았다. 하나는 이번이 마지막이라는, 감방 가지 않게만 도와달라는 남동생의 문자. '누나 그동안 알게 모르게 벌어둔 거 내가 모르지 않거든' 따위 말만 덧붙이지 않았어도 맘이 움직일 뻔했다. 그다음, 아버지의 검사 결과와 검사비 24만 원이 찍힌 영수증의 사진 파일은 엄마가 보낸 거였다. 다음 문자는 큰형님한테서 왔다. 내일모레 제사에 몇 시까지 올 수 있느냐는 물음이었다. 예 형님, 저 아이들 학교 보낸 다음 바로 찾

not sure if entirely "non-risky" materials is possible among living things, other than plants, but at least the book had no intense desire, no wild enthusiasms, and no violence. It reminded me of those "morally healthy" songs that were included as the last tracks on LPs by Korean singers in earlier days of repression. But a tale about a group of reformed boys winning a basketball tournament seemed like a cliché aimed at people's emotions, which made me think that P.C. was trying to take the easy route, and such a clean-cut story and characters were evidence of the writer's lack of a will to try something new or to reflect on or change the reality.

On the other hand, a lot of people must need a story like that, or else that "fairytale" would not have been published in the first place. Some people who are chronic victims must take such a "safe" narrative as a relief; they don't wish to read about grief or suffering in novels... Some of P.C.'s devoted readers were disappointed in the lack of style, which had been prominent in the author's earlier works—the unexpected laughter amid cynicism, the subtle smiles within loud laughter. "I like calm and gentle stories, too, but in P.C.'s previous works there was tension along with serenity. Now the stories are nothing more than smooth and bland,

아뵐게요. 아이들은 학원까지 마치고 저녁때 시간 맞춰 오도록 할 거고요. 전송 아이콘을 클릭하고 마지막 문자를 열었다. 정말로 다 없던 일로 해도 괜찮으시겠어요? 선생님 의향을 존중할 거고요, 기지급된 계약금 200만 원을 저희 쪽에 따로 돌려주실 필요는 없으세요.

거기에는 답장을 보내지 않은 채 좀 이따 하교할 아이들의 간식거리를 준비하기 위해 일어났다. 문득 다시 펼쳐보지 않을 책들의 일렬로 늘어선 등을 손가락으로 훑으며 방을 나섰다. 돌보아야 할 남편과 아이들, 엄마 아빠 동생까지 있는데 유일하게 나한테 없는 건 아내였다…… 펜 끝에서 한번 번져나가기 시작한 말들이 그리는 궤적을 바라보는 일은 나름대로 의미 있었다. 그러나 내가 지금까지 해온 일들은 흘러가는 말들을 포착하여 언제 부서져도 이상하지 않은 물방울의 표면에 새겨나가는 일이었는지도 모른다. 그리하여 지금은 원래의 가장 올바른 자리로 돌아가기에, 그리고 말의 죽음을 맞이하기에 가장 적절한 시간일 뿐이다.

feel-good tales. I guess there's nothing more to get here. I'm done reading them. I think perhaps he should stop writing..."

Since people often hide unexpected and sharp razor blades, though, not even this feel-good story, which didn't make it anywhere near lists of bestsellers, could avoid slicing and dicing. The five basketball players were juvenile delinquents who had been charged with serious crimes: assault and injury, robbery, attempted rape. Some people complained that the people who had suffered from their crimes weren't mentioned, let alone featured, thereby erasing their existence. Others exclaimed how unbelievable it was that criminals who had tormented people could now evoke readers' tears while playing sports. And still others questioned whether the boys had the right to become happy and win a trophy, and whether they'd ever apologized to their victims instead of having "reflection time," and whether it was wrong to have characters who hadn't served jail time for their crimes but only lived in a juvenile delinquent center, turn into heroes.

The author might have thought that the novel was an attempt to shine light on children in dark places; but by doing so P.C. seemed to fail to give voice to those who were suffering in even darker places.

Moreover, by adding a trite backdrop for each child, including an alcoholic father and ailing or runaway mother, the writer perhaps wanted to give them an easy justification by providing a troubled early environment, from which they would understandably turn to crime. And, as usual, there was criticism of P.C. as intent to describe women as irresponsible parents, since it was always the mothers who left the family. And, some people asked, would the publisher please stop trying to make money on stories about people's pain and suffering by putting a pretty cover on them?

Around that time, P.C.'s account was finally locked, although, by then, out of 50,000 followers, only about 5,000 were still following it. And it was deleted entirely a few days, after the latest book was removed from bookstores. Since this last novel wasn't as popular, though, not a lot of people noticed or ridiculed P.C.'s disappearance. None of them asked about the author on the publisher's account, and it didn't seem as though the publisher was making efforts to look into P.C.'s whereabouts. But I knew that P.C. had quit writing and eased into just daily life or hobbies—that the author would become someone who wandered in the forest of insufficient words, and no one would be able to find traces of P.C. ever again.

I closed my browser and checked four text messages that had arrived. First was a message from my younger brother, who promised me that this was the last time he would do something bad—so could I please help him stay out of jail by bailing him out? I was almost moved until I read his following words: "I know that you saved up, here and there, so don't think that I don't know you have the money." The next text was from my mother: a photo of a 240,000-won receipt from the hospital and my father's test results. The third was from my sister-in-law asking me what time I was planning to come to prepare for an ancestral memorial service. I replied that I would be there right after sending the kids off to school, and that they would come after their cram-school sessions in the evening. After sending that text, I opened the last one: Would it really be okay to just forget the whole thing? We will certainly respect your opinion on this matter. You don't have to return the two million-won advance for the book to us.

Without sending a reply to that message, I got up to make snacks for the children, who were due back from school. Then, after running my fingers along the spines of books arranged in a line on a shelf, I left the room. I had a husband, children, mother, father, and younger brother to care for... But it's true: I didn't have a wife. It had been rather meaningful for me to observe the words that flowed from the end of my pen. But perhaps what I'd done was merely capture the flowing words and scratch them onto the surface of water drops, which could disappear at any second. Therefore, now might be the best time for me to return to my rightful place and accept the death of words.

# 창작노트
# Writer's Note

그럼에도 불구하고 나의 이 소설이 현재의 혼란이, 나 자신뿐 아니라 어떤 이들에게 혹여 그럴듯하거나 편리한 알리바이로 작용하지는 않기를.

어쩌면 오래전 습작 시절부터 줄곧 계속되어온 답 없는 고민이었을 것이다. 몇 편의 소설을 꾸준히 돌려 읽은 동료들이, 너는 왜 소설 속에서 자꾸 사람을 죽이니? 물었을 때부터였을 것이다. 그들의 뉘앙스는 비난이 아니었고 오히려 그 말들에는 가벼운 우스갯소리에 가까운 에코가 입혀졌다.

떠올려보면 그 질문에는 여러 다른 의도가 담겼을 수

Nevertheless, I do hope this short story, the current state of confusion, do not become a plausible or convenient alibi for me or for others.

It is an issue I have mulled over, without arriving at a solution, since before my debut as a professional writer. It probably started when my colleagues read several of my works and asked: Why do you keep killing people in your stories? The sense of the question was not critical, though, but rather had a feeling of humoring.

When I think back on it, however, perhaps that question contained other intentions: Concern that an ending with death would make my stories too

도 있다. 인물의 사망 엔딩이라면 지난번과 형식이 똑같아지지 않느냐는 우려, 혹시 평소 일상의 개인적 원한을 곳곳에 깊이 품고 살아서 창작으로 해소(심리학에서 '승화'라고 일컫는 바로 그 행위)하느냐는 의문 같은 것들.

글이 쌓여나가는 동안, 소설 속에서 작가가 죽인 인물들에 대한 책임감을 느껴야 할 것 같다는 생각이 어렴풋이 들었으나, 누군가가 소설 속에서 죽음을 맞이한다면 그럴 만한 이유가 있다고—그 일은 서사적 필요에 의해서만 발생하며 소설 속 인물들은 실존하지 않으므로 그들에게 죄의식까지 갖는다면 그건 죄의식이라기보다는 작가 개인의 자의식에 불과한 포즈라고 여겼다.

물론 '서사적 필요'라는 근거 또한, 인물을 조립식 완구처럼 컨베이어벨트 곳곳에 기계적으로 배치함으로써 스토리의 원자화/파편화로 문학의 본령을 해친다고 비판받을 가능성을 언제나 품고 있기는 했지만, 그것은 또 다른 맥락의 이야기가 되겠다.

누군가가 내 소설을 읽고 고통스러워한다. 고통의 이유는 제각각이다. 자기 어린 시절이 생각나서, 비슷한 경험을 한 적이 있어서, 그런데 그 경험들이 대체로 옳

similar in form to my previous ones, or curiosity about whether killing characters was a way to release my own anger over grudges (dubbed "sublimation" in psychology).

As my writings increased, I had a vague impression that I should feel responsible for the people I had killed off in my works. But I ignored it, thinking that death often occurred in fiction for a good reason: the logical necessity of the narrative. And since fictional characters don't exist in reality, the "guilt" a writer might feel over their deaths is not really guilt, but merely a facade that is only the writer's self-awareness.

Certainly, it's true that even the rationale of narrative necessity is always prone to the criticism that, by arranging and manipulating characters like toys assembled on a conveyor belt, I was fragmenting the narrative, and thereby ruining the essential nature of literature. But this is a discussion for another time.

Some people are pained when they read my stories. And they have their reasons: because they remember their own childhoods; because they've experienced similar events that were wrong or vi-

지 못하고 폭력적이어서. 때론 소설 속 상황과 인물들의 환난이 불쾌하고 싫어서.

그렇다면 나는 그들의 고통에 어디까지 책임을 느껴야 할까. 나는 혹시 누군가를 도구화했나. 나는 가공의 인물들을 내 소설에 배우로 등장시켜서 아낌없이 쓰고 내다 버렸나.

사람들이 의문을 갖기 시작했다. 이런 불행한 일을 한꺼번에 겪는 사람이 세상에 어디 있어?(있다. 왜 없겠어. 보통은 더 많이 겪지. 원래 행운이 산발적으로 어쩌다가 온다면, 불행은 뻥 뚫린 고속도로로 몰아닥친다.) 주인공을 이렇게까지 학대해야만 하는 이유가 뭐지? 인물에 대한 푸대접이 정도가 지나쳐서 불쾌한데.(내가 아는 문학은 언제나 지나친 것, 과한 것, 따라서 '그 너머'에 존재하므로 여기에 현존하는 내 손으로는 쥘 수 없는 어떤 것이었다.)

한번 생각하기 시작하자, 해서는 안 될 것 같은 일들의 목록이 생겨났다. 소설 속에서 누구도 맞거나 때리거나 폭언을 주고받으면 안 되었다. 그 어떤 귀한 물건이나 자존심을 훔치거나 박탈당해서는 안 되었고 죽거나 죽이거나 해서는 더더욱 안 되었다. 문제될 소지를

olent; because they dislike the situations and difficulties the characters face and find them to be uncomfortable.

How much responsibility should I take upon myself for their pain? Did I inadvertently turn people into instruments? Did I make characters into important people in order to manipulate them, and in the end discard them?

People began to ask questions like: Who experiences so many difficulties at the same time? (Answer: There are people who do. Usually, many more than we think or know about. Luck arrives sporadically, but misfortune comes sweeping through on a highway.) Why does the author need to abuse the main character so much? The writer's cruel treatment of the characters makes me uncomfortable. (As far as I know, literature is excessive, extravagant, and exists somewhere "beyond," and therefore is ungraspable with my own hands.)

Once I started thinking about these questions concerning the suffering of my characters, I discovered there was a list of things I couldn't do. No one in my stories should hit or be beaten or exchange verbal abuses. No one should steal precious items

애당초 근절하고 싶다면 어떤 불편한 상황이나 혐오를 배제하고, 누군가가 부당한 취급을 받아서는 안 되었다. 그 경우 꼭 그래야만 하는 서사적 근거와 작가적 이유와, 경우에 따라서는 공공의 동의마저 작동해야 했(다고까지 느꼈)으며, 근거가 있다 한들 그것이 얼마나 합당한지의 기준은 사람마다 달랐으므로, 한 편의 소설 속 공간이 누구도 코를 틀어막거나 눈살 찌푸리지 않는 무균실이 되는 일이란 불가능했다.

그럼에도 모든 소거법을 적용하고 나면, 친환경적이고 도덕이 살아 숨 쉬며 정치적으로 올바르고 인간애가 넘치는 한편 사회적으로 최선의 합의가 이루어진(그런게 실제로 존재하는지는 우선 접어두고), 요컨대 큰 무리 없이 공공선을 이룩하는 이야기가 나올 수도 있을 것 같았다. 그러나 내가 알고 있는 세계는 그렇게 매끈하지 않았고, 인간은 존재하는 한 서로가 서로에게 공해라는 내 생각에는 지각변동이 일어나지 않았다. 따라서 나는 계속 무리수를 두기로 했는데, 그러면서도 생활인으로서의 자아는, 인간으로 태어나 그래선 안 된다고 훈수를 두면서 어디까지가 피치 못할 표현이자 묘사인지를 묻고 있었다. 어느 한쪽의 목소리도 무시할 수 없다는

or pride from someone or have them stolen from themselves, much less kill or be killed. In order to eliminate the smallest details that could turn out to be problematic, I would have to remove all uncomfortable situations and hatred, and made sure no one would be treated unfairly. If I wanted to include any of the above negative occurrences, I felt I needed to provide narrative evidence, authorial reasons, and (even) public consensus at times. But even if I were to provide my reasons, since people have different standards of reasonableness, it would be impossible to create an aseptic room for a story in which no one would frown or hold their noses.

It seemed that it might be possible to create a story that was eco-friendly, ethical, politically correct, full of humanity, and contained the best possible social compromises (putting aside the thought that such a reality does not exist)—in other words, to create a story that promoted the greater good without problems. But the world I knew was not smooth and gentle. And no tectonic activity has occurred to change my belief that humans are toxic to other humans. Therefore I decided to continue to push the boundaries. My conscience was telling me that I shouldn't, since I was born a human; but at

생각에 강박적으로 귀를 기울이고 반영했으며, 그러다 보니 나는 퍽 일관성 없는 사람이 되었지만, 그래도 한 번 더 생각하고 고민한다는 일련의 프로세스가 추가된 것 자체에 의의를 두는 형편이다.

이 소설은 해결되지 않은, 현재진행형의, 사람과 사람이 공존하는 한 영원히 일도양단되지 않는 질문과 그로 인한 혼란의 부산물이다. 결론을 내리지 못했으므로 결과물 아닌 부산물이라 쓴다. 혼란이라는 두 글자를 함께 적었으나 보는 이에 따라 변명 내지는 자기합리화로 읽히기도 할 것이다.

인간사는 디즈니풍의 애니메이션이 아니며 소설은 기계가 아닌 생물이어서 내가 수습할 수 없는 어떤 세계를 향해 나아가고 있는데, 그곳이 대다수의 정직하고 선량하며 공평무사한 구성원들이 원하는 바로 거기인지는 알 수 없다. 그런 세계에서 우리는 어디까지 근엄해지고 어디까지 올발라질 수 있을까. 분명한 건 내 소설이 그러지는 못할 것 같다는 예감뿐이다.

the same time it was asking me how far was too far in describing or expressing something. Since I couldn't simply ignore either one of these attitudes, I obsessed about trying to reflect both ideas in my stories, and, as a result, I became inconsistent. But I decided to find meaning in the fact that I was adding another step of thinking and taking things into consideration in the process of writing.

This story is the result of that unresolved and ongoing questioning and the ensuing chaos—as long as people exist. Since I was unable to reach a conclusion, I would say it is not an outcome but a by-product. (I have just written "chaos," but, depending on the reader, it could be viewed as "excuse" or "self-justification.")

The history of mankind is not a Disney animation, and fiction is not mechanical but organic. Fiction leads into a world that I cannot control, yet I also don't know if that world is one that most honest, good, just people want. In such a world, how serious and how righteous can people become? The only thing that is obvious to me is a hunch that my works are probably not headed for that world.

# 해설
# Commentary

# 입장의 소설: 소설에 의한, 소설을 위한, 소설의 정치적 올바름에 대하여

소영현 (문학평론가)

구병모의 소설은, 좀 이상하게 들릴 수도 있지만, 분류하자면 청각형 소설에 가깝다. 소리 내어 읽기에 적합하다. 아니 (귀로) 듣기에 더 적합하다. 소리 내어 읽으면 말하는 자의 음색이 분별되고 윤곽이 떠오른다. 문체가 만들어내는 음악성이나 그에 따른 가독성에 대한 상찬으로 오해될 수 있으나, 구병모의 소설은 언제나 냉소를 품고 길게 늘어선 만연체의 문장으로 이루어져 있다. 구병모 소설을 채우는 것은 단어나 문장이 아니라 말이다. 말로 이루어진 구병모 소설의 개성은 그 말이 육성으로 전해진 말이라는 점에 놓인다. 굳이 덧붙이자면 구병모의 소설은 청각형 소설이자 읽는 자를

# The Spell of a Story: On the Political Correctness of Fiction, by Fiction, and for Fiction

So Young-hyun (literary critic)

Although it might seem odd to say so to some people, Gu Byeong-mo's works, if I were to categorize them, are auditory fiction. They're good for reading out loud. Or, actually, they're even better for listening to. When something is read out loud, you have the sound of the speaker's voice and can picture their silhouette. This is not to mistake what I'm saying as merely praise for the musicality or readability of Gu's style—her short stories and novels are always made up of lengthy sentences that harbor cynicism. Yet these stories do not consist so much of words or sentences, but of speeches. If I were to elaborate, I would say they are auditory

'말하기-듣기' 구도로 끌어들이는 대화형 소설이다.

구병모 소설에 두루 해당하지만, 특히 육성으로 말하는 자의 면모가 두드러진 소설 「이창」(『그것이 나만은 아니기를』, 문학과지성사, 2015)이나 「어느 피씨주의자의 종생기」(『창작과비평』 2017년 여름호)에서 이러한 성격은 뚜렷하다. 「어느 피씨주의자의 종생기」의 돋보이는 개성이 여기서 마련되고 있기도 하다. 기발하거나 신기한 이야기들이 흥미롭게 전개되지만, 구병모의 소설 세계를 만능 이야기꾼이 쉼 없이 만들어내는 이야기의 다발로만 단정 지을 수 없는 이유다. 돌이켜보면 한국소설은 감각에 관한 한 (작가 혹은 독자의) 시각의 단련에 주력해온 편이다. 존재하지만 보이지 않는 영역이나 존재에 대한 새로운 조명과 다른 묘사법의 개발에 힘써온 것이다. 시선의 전능성 자체에 대한 의심이 전면적으로 이루어지지는 않으며, 시선이 놓인 자리에 대한 질문도 그리 많지 않다. 시선에 대한 다각도의 모색이 이루어지는 반면 시선의 위치성에 대한 성찰은 의외로 많지 않은 것이다.

구병모 소설에서 화자-인물의 신뢰성은 소설 전체로 보면 언제나 재고된다. 빠져들기보다 한 걸음 물러서게

and conversational narratives, pulling in the reader to "listen" to the "talking" narrator.

Although this characteristic occurs in most of Gu's works, vocal narrators are particularly prominent in two of her short stories: "Rear Window" (included in *Hopefully Not Just Me*, Moonji Publishing, 2015) and "The Story of P.C." (published in *Ch'angjak kwa pip'yong*, 2017 Summer). This is also the root of the individuality in "The Story of P.C." Intriguing and ingenious stories unfold in interesting ways; yet Gu Byeong-mo's works are more than a bouquet of narratives continuously spun by a great storyteller. In terms of the senses, Korean fiction has been devoted to either the writer's or reader's sense of vision, focused on bringing to light invisible areas or existences or developing different methods of description. The omnipotent gaze tends not to be doubted, and there aren't many questions about the intended target of the gaze. While multifaceted approaches have been tried, to examine the gazing, we have rarely reflected on the positionality of the gaze.

In Gu's works, though, the reliability of the narrator-character is always reexamined. Instead of pulling in the reader, this allows the reader to take a step back. But this distance does not result from

한다. 그러나 조성된 거리는 정상성을 벗어난 존재들의 근원적 결핍이나 결함에 의한 것이 아니다. 그 혹은 그녀의 말에 진정성이나 신빙성이 부족해서도 아니다. 그 말의 진위 여부는 말하는 자의 말이 놓인 위치성에서 온다. 깨어 있는 시민임을 자부하는 한 가정주부가 아파트 거실 창밖 이웃집에서 벌어지는 아동폭력 사태에 적극적으로 개입하는 과정을 다룬 소설 「이창」이 보여주었듯, 작가의 관심은 사건이나 사태의 진위 여부나 그것이 은폐한 허위성에 대한 폭로가 아니다. 오히려 전적으로 호의에서 시작된 사회적 개입 행위가 '고의는 아니지만' 타인의 삶에 대한 침해이거나 심각한 해악일 수 있음을 환기하는 데 있다. 사회적으로 합의된 도덕이나 자율적으로 구축된 윤리 등이 일상에서 태도로서 구현된 정치적 올바름이라는 것도 사람들의 관계 속에서 각자의 입장에 따라 의도와는 다른 의미를 만들어낼 수 있음을 보여주고자 하는 것이다.

말하는 자의 음색과 윤곽은 구병모 소설에서 이야기 자체보다 말하는 자(화자-인물)의 위치성을 의식하게 하는 주요한 장치다. 이 위치성이란 말하는 자의 말에 상대적 관점을 부여하고 그 말에 다른 이해의 가능성을

a fundamental lack or from flaws in characters who are beyond normal. Nor does it result from a lack in their sincerity or credibility. The truths of the words spoken by the characters in Gu's works are determined by the positionality of the words. In "Rear Window," for instance, a housewife who claims to be an engaged person actively intervenes in a child abuse incident. Yet Gu's interest is not in the incident or figuring out or exposing a hidden truth or falsehood; rather, it is in pointing out that an act of social intervention that began out of goodwill could end up violating another person's privacy or becoming a serious malaise. The author attempts to show that "political correctness," motivated by a desire to promote socially shared morals and voluntary ethics—this concept that has entered common usage—can become something less salutary in the relationship among people, depending on their positionings.

The vocal quality and outline of the speaker are important mechanisms for making the reader mindful of the position of the speaker-narrator, rather than focusing on the story itself. I use the term "positionality" here to mean the reflexivity that Gu's stories acquire, in that the reader attributes a

열어둔다는 점에서, 구병모 소설이 확보한 성찰성의 다른 말이다. 애초에 전적으로 옳거나 그른 것이 있다고는 믿지 않는, 작가의 세계에 대한 유연한 이해법은 소설 속에 펼쳐진 이야기 전체를 어떤 의미에서 진위나 선악의 판단정지 영역에 놓이게 한다. 소설 자체가 이러저러한 판정들이 다면적으로 중첩된 시공간이 되기도 한다. 이것을 가능하게 하는 힘은 구병모 소설이 형식화한 성찰성, 말하는 자의 말과 그 말에 거리를 두게 하는 장치가 만들어내는 특유의 균형감에서 온다.「어느 피씨주의자의 종생기」말미에 제시된 문자 메시지의 반전 효과는 소설에 의견으로서의 위치성/성찰성을 부여한다.

작가의 이해법을 빌려 말하자면 성찰성이 자체로 옳거나 그른 것은 아니다. 시공간적 조건과 무관하게 우리의 삶에서 언제나 필요조건인 것도 아니다. 소설이 삶을 위한 미래적 가치를 담지하거나 혹은 소설적 몸피로서 구현하는 일이 소설의 존재론적 당위가 될 필요는 없는 것이다. 그럼에도 구병모 소설이 담지한 성찰성은 유의미하다. 성찰성은 극단적 개인화 경향이 삶의 미세한 국면에까지 영향을 드리운 이 시대에 적극적으로 요

relative perspective to the words of the speaker and understands that their words are open to different interpretations. This flexible understanding of the world, created by an author who does not believe in absolute right or wrong, situates the entire narrative in a space in which truth, or good or evil, cannot be judged. The fiction becomes a time and space woven in layers of judgments on all sides. What makes this possible is the reflexivity formalized in Gu's fiction, the balance created by the mechanism of distancing the speaker's words from them. For instance, the text message that reveals the twist at the end of "The Story of P.C." seals the reflexivity of the story, positioning the narrative as an opinion.

In Gu's way of understanding, reflexivity in itself is not right or wrong. It is not an absolute necessity in our lives, regardless of the temporal-spatial conditions in which we find ourselves. Fiction does not contain future-oriented values in life, and the act of writing fiction does not have to be the justification for the existence of fiction. Yet the reflexivity in Gu's fiction is significant because it is a future-oriented value, and is also an attitude that is needed in this world, in which the tendency toward

청되는 미래적 가치이자 삶의 태도이기 때문이다.

소설의 윤리를 둘러싼 논란과 이후 여파를 다룬 소설 「어느 피씨주의자의 종생기」는 명백하게 2015년 여름 이후 한국문단에 불어 닥친 일련의 사태에 대한 작가의 응답으로 보인다. 문단을 대표하는 한 작가의 표절 의혹에서 시작되어 #문단_내_성폭력 고발 사태로까지 이어진 추문들은 문단의 구조적 문제들과의 관련 속에서 새로운 논의 지평을 마련하고 있으며, 창작과 비평의 자리에서 문학과 윤리의 문제로 곱씹어지고 있다. 문학적으로 중요하게 다루어져야 할 문제이지만 '문학적으로' 하나의 의견이나 태도를 표명하는 일은 결코 쉬운 일이 아니다. 구병모는 「어느 피씨주의자의 종생기」를 통해 논란의 발원지이자 폭발적 영향력을 만들어낸 소셜네트워크의 성격을 놓치지 않으면서 한국문단이 처한 사태를 폭넓은 시야에서 알레고리화한다.

「어느 피씨주의자의 종생기」는, 지속적으로 신간을 선보이며 꾸준한 판매 지수를 유지하던 한 작가가 사회에 대한 관심을 드러낸 신작의 내용을 둘러싼 논란에 휩싸이게 된 후, 논란에 대처하는 출판사와 작가의 면모를 추적한다. 작가가 휩싸인 논란은 사회파 스릴러로

extreme individualism influences even the most trivial aspects of our lives. Dealing as it does with the ethics of novels, "The Story of P.C." seems to be responding to the avalanche of events that shook the Korean literary world during and after the summer of 2015, starting with an allegation of plagiarism against a well-established writer, and going on to the issue of #sexual_abuse_within_lit_circle. These scandals have opened up a new arena for the examination of structural problems in the literary world in Korea, and have prompted reflections on the issues of creating literature and ethics.

Nevertheless, although these are important issues that need to be addressed, it is not easy to express opinions or attitudes *within* literature. Through "The Story of P.C." Gu addresses the problems faced by the Korean literary world and turns them into an allegory, while also not neglecting the explosive nature of social media sites—those breeding grounds of controversies.

"The Story of P.C." follows a writer who publishes a book every year and has a steady following and the writer's publisher, as they respond to a controversy surrounding the author's latest work about social issues. The controversy that embroils the writer is ethical, specifically concerning the writer's

분류할 수 있는 신작에 대한 윤리적 비난으로, 구체적으로는 소설에 등장하는 불법체류 외국인 노동자, 결혼이주 방글라데시 여성, 미모의 청각 장애인에 대한 소설가의 태도 즉 소설가의 사회적 타자에 대한 정치적 올바름의 문제에 관한 것이다. 논란의 내용이 아니라 논란에 대처하는 작가의 태도와 논란의 경과에 주목하게 하는 것은 작품이 획득한 알레고리로서의 힘과 연관된다. 작가 P씨를 둘러싼 논란은, 논란이 일고 논란의 당사자가 진정성을 담은 해명에 '뒤늦게' 나서지만 사태가 진정되기보다 악화된다. 논란 자체는 비웃음과 맹비난이 거셌다가 관심이 식어버리는 과정 속에서 어느새 흐지부지되고 만다. 이 과정에서 윤리적 비난은 점차 논란의 당사자 뿐 아니라 주변이나 논란에 입장을 표명한 모든 이들에게로 번지게 된다.

결과 편으로 갈리면서 극단적인 대결구도로 치닫게 되는 이 논란의 종생기를 추적하면서 구병모는 SNS 상에서의 많은 논란들이 어떻게 증폭되고 소멸하는가를 보여주는 동시에 논란의 치명적 여파를 날카롭게 짚는다. 「어느 피씨주의자의 종생기」에서 논란의 여파가 얼마나 폭력적인 것인가는 이후 작가 P씨가 신작을 출간

attitude toward the characters in the book: an illegal foreign laborer, a Bangladeshi woman who came to Korea as a marriage migrant, and a beautiful woman with a hearing impairment. In other words, the short story is about a novelist's political correctness toward "others" in our society. Instead of focusing on the controversy, though, Gu addresses the author's attitude and the progress of the controversy, using the allegorical power of story. The writer, referred to only as "P.C.," offers a belated yet sincere apology after the controversy, but matters still worsen instead of improving. The controversy itself fizzles out as people's interest dies down. However, in this process, ethical criticisms against the writer spread to criticisms of the publisher and critics and to everyone who expresses their opinion on the controversy.

Tracing the path through this controversy, in which people take sides and stand their ground in extreme opposition, Gu shows how controversies are amplified and obscured in the social media and makes an incisive point about the critical aftermath of such controversies. The reader only realizes the extent of this aftermath after P.C. publishes another book containing "fewer problematic characters and situations," with storylines that can be described as

하고 나서야 확인된다. 작가 P씨의 차기작들은 점차 "문제적 인물이나 상황"은 줄었으나 "큰 굴곡 없이 평탄하다 가끔 완만한 곡선을 그린 뒤 제자리로 안착하는" 소설이 되고, "더 이상 어떤 새로운 시도나 현실 반영 내지는 현실 변용을 하려는 의욕"을 찾기 어려운 소설이 되어버린다. 그 여파가 작가 P씨의 작가로서의 생이 끝날 때까지 이어진다는 사실의 환기는 의미심장하다.

구병모 작가가 전망하는 논란의 사후적 영향은 소설과 삶 사이의 간극이 사라지고 소설이 삶 쪽으로 납작해지면서 결국 작가로서의 삶이 소멸되고 마는, 결과적으로 삶 자체의 협소화로 귀결되는 나쁜 결말이다. 그러나 그것은, 작품이 세심하게 짚고 있듯 작가 P씨의 무능이라기보다 현실과 허구, 삶과 소설 사이의 본래적 간극 때문이다. "소설로 누군가를 다치게 할 생각은 지금도 앞으로도 없"다는 작가 P씨의 (윤리적) 의도가 좌절되는 것은 "누군가가 조금 불편하더라도 소설의 개연성과 완성도에 집중하는" 소설의 윤리, 즉 재현 자체의 폭력성에 의해서이다. 소설을 둘러싼 정치적 올바름 논란이 불러온 창작물의 변천사 혹은 소설의 몰락기라 할 만한 「어느 피씨주의자의 종생기」는 이렇게 결국 소설

"a gradual arc without much fluctuation landing within the range of what is socially acceptable," and where it is difficult to find the "will to try something new or to reflect or change reality." The fact that such criticisms continue until P.C.'s life as a novelist is finally over is highly significant.

The aftermath of such controversies, as Gu Byeong-mo predicts, leads to a narrowed life, in which the distance between fiction and life disappears, with fiction forced into the realm of life and flattened, and until ultimately the life of a novelist is crushed. Yet, as is keenly pointed out in the story, this does not occur due to the writer's incompetence but rather because of the intrinsic gap between reality and fiction, between life and made-up stories. P.C.'s (ethical) intention "not to hurt people" with her fictional works becomes frustrated due to the "ethics" of fiction, which demands that a novelist focus on plausibility and completion in the novel "even if it might make some people a bit uncomfortable." In other words, the ethics of fiction is involved in the violence inherent in the process of representation.

"The Story of P.C.," a narrative of the transformation of creative works and the end of fiction brought on by controversies over literature and

이란 무엇인가, 삶과 소설은 어떻게 같고 또 다른가라는 질문을 불러온다. 아니 소설이 삶 쪽으로 무한히 가까워질 수 있으나 삶 자체가 될 수는 없으며 오히려 그 간극인 소설적 결함이 역설적으로 삶의 허점을 들여다보게 하는 것이 아닌가를 반문한다. 「어느 피씨주의자의 종생기」는 소설의 이름을 다시 쓰고 소설의 범주를 넓히는 방법론 자체에 천착한 소설이면서, 동시에 소설이란 독자대중을 통해 발현된 시대정신 혹은 우리 시대의 문화적 한계치가 만드는 것이자 그 과정 자체임을 보여준 소설이다.

각도를 바꿔 말하자면, 구병모의 「어느 피씨주의자의 종생기」는 문학의 윤리에 대한 작가로서의 고민을 흥미로운 이야기로 구현한 소설이다. 한국문단이 직면한 사태의 본질을 짚고, 독자대중이 새롭게 부각된 사정과 그것이 창작에 미치는 영향을 성찰한다. 또한 점차 SNS의 영향력이 현실을 견인하게 되는 사정에 대한 하나의 이야기이자 (온라인상의) 윤리적 논란이 (오프라인에) 야기한 폭력적 결과에 대한 작가의 묵직한 발언이다. 무엇보다 육성의 말하는 자라는 장치를 통해 그 발언을 한나 아렌트가 상정했던 바로 그런 말할 권리를 행사하

political correctness, brings us to the questions: What is fiction? And how do life and fiction differ or not differ? This short story retorts by arguing that fiction can come close to life, but cannot be it, and that the "flaws" in fiction, which are the gap between fiction and life, lead people to examine the flaws in life. "The Story of P.C." redefines fiction and delves into the possible methodology for broadening the range of fiction. At the same time, it shows that fiction is a process and an outcome of the cultural limitations and spirit of the time expressed through the reading public.

From the writer's perspective, "The Story of P.C." is an engaging means of illustrating her thoughts on the ethics of literature. It also points out the crux of a problem the Korean literary world is facing, explores the manner in which the reading public has newly emerged, and reflects on how this has influenced writers' creations. Furthermore, it is a story about how the social media's influence has begun to spearhead reality. It is the author's sobering statement on the radical outcome in the offline world brought on by an online ethical controversy. Above all, through a speaker, Gu turns her own statement into that of a character exercising her right to free speech. Combining all these aspects

는 존재/자리의 것으로 만든다. 이 모든 것의 융합물인 이 소설의 소중한 미덕은, 현실에서 벌어진 논란을 소설적으로 구성하고, 위치성과 성찰성을 담지한 목소리(육성으로 말하는 자)로 한국사회와 한국문학이 직면한 윤리의 문제에 관한 경청할 만한 묵직한 의견을 표명하는, 바로 그 자리에 있다. 「어느 피씨주의자의 종생기」는 사유가 아니라 사유의 위치성을 밝히는 '입장으로서의 소설'이라는 새로운 영역의 발견이다.

**소영현** 2005년 연세대학교 국어국문학과에서 박사학위를 받았고, 2003년 계간 《작가세계》에서 비평활동을 시작했다. 지은 책으로 『문학청년의 탄생』(푸른역사, 2008), 『부랑청년 전성시대』(푸른역사, 2008), 『분열하는 감각들』(문학과지성사, 2010), 『프랑켄슈타인 프로젝트』(봄아필, 2013), 『하위의 시간』(문학동네, 2016), 『올빼미의 숲』(문학과지성사, 2017), 공저로는 『감정의 인문학』(봄아필, 2013), 『문학사 이후의 문학사』(푸른역사, 2013), 『감성사회』(글항아리, 2014) 등이 있다. 현재 연세대 국학연구원 HK연구교수로 있다.

and attributes, the virtue of this short story is that it discusses real-life controversies in literature and makes a serious statement about the problems of ethics that Korean society and literature are facing through a voice with a particular stance and reflexivity. Thus, "The Story of P.C." is not a contemplation but a discovery of new literary territory—a "short story as a position"—that determines the positioning of the writer's reflections.

**So Young-hyun** So Young-hyun received a Ph.D. in Korean language and literature and began her career as a literary critic in 2003, when she published an article in the quarterly literary magazine *Jakga segye*. Her publications include *The Birth of the Literary Youth* (2008), *The Hey-Day of Young Tramps* (2008), *Fragmenting Senses* (2010), *The Frankenstein Project* (2013), *Subordinate Times* (2016), and *Owl Forests* (2017), as well as co-authoring *Humanities of Sentiment* (2013), *History of Literature After the History of Literature* (2013), and *Society of Emotions* (2014).

# 비평의 목소리
# Critical Acclaim

구병모의 스토리에 개입하는 판타지는 유별난 경험이나 기발한 상상력에서 기인한 게 아니다. 그것은 당연하게도, 그가 세상을 읽는 태도에서, 세상의 모순과 교착을 감각하는 어떤 문학적 촉수에서 발생한다. 이해할 수 있는 것과 이해할 수 없는 것을 함께 감당하려는 지적 성실함과 정서적 진솔함을 통해 그것은 형상화된다. 빛은 빛이고 어둠은 어둠이라고 생각하는 자, 보이는 것과 보는 것이 동일하다고 믿는 자, 세계의 밤은 어디에나 있다는 것을 알지 못하는 자들에게는 구병모의 소설이 그다지 흥미롭지 않을 수도 있다. 그러나 이 세계에서 우리의 욕망은 끝내 끝까지 드러나지 못함에 우울했던 자, 그러면서도 현실이라는 무대에서 이미 환상이라는 쇼를 보고

Fantasy in Gu Byeong-mo's stories do not originate from particular experiences or her ingenious creativity. Rather, it comes from the way in which she reads the world—from her literary antennae that sense the contradictions and intricacies of the world. And it is expressed through her intellectual earnestness to handle both what can and cannot be understood as well as through emotional honesty. People who believe that light is light and darkness is darkness, as well as people who do not know that the night of the world can be found everywhere and anywhere might not find Gu's fiction interesting. But those who are depressed because people's desires

있는 자들이라면, 구병모의 짧은 이야기들에서도 몇 차례씩 오싹한 쾌감을 맛보게 될 것이다.

백지은, 「즐거운 왜상(歪像)들: 구병모 소설 읽기」,
《자음과모음》, 자음과모음, 2011.

활달한 환상의 서사에도 불구하고 구병모의 소설은 전통적인 단편 미학에 충실한 듯 느껴진다. 흥미로운 사건을 중심으로 치밀하게 서사가 직조되어 나가고, 그 과정에서 주제의식이 명료하게 드러난다. 이야기의 재미와 힘이 충분히 살아있으며, 묘사와 상징 못지않게 세계의 폐부를 정면으로 겨냥하는 날카로운 입담도 인상적이다. 무엇보다 매우 일상적인 감각에 바탕한 세계의 풍경은 리얼리티의 구체성과 호소력을 확보하고 있다.

권채린, 「푸리아의 후예들」, 《내일을 여는 작가》, 한국작가회의, 2011.

are never fully realized, yet are still watching the show of illusions on the stage of reality would be able to taste the thrill and pleasures more than once in Gu's short stories.

Baek Ji-eun, "Pleasant anamorphoses: Reading Gu Byungmo's fiction," Jaeum and Moeum, *Jaeum and Moeum* Publishing, 2011.

Despite the vigorously fantastical narrative, Gu Byeong-mo's story feels as though it is faithful to the aesthetics of traditional short stories: the narrative is thoroughly woven around an interesting event, and the theme of the story is presented in a clear way. The story is fun and powerful, and along with descriptions and symbols it contains and impressively poignant words that take a clear aim at the heart of the world. Above all, her view of the world, which is based on very ordinary insights, is realistically concrete and appealing.

Kwon Chae-rin, "The descendants of Furia," *Writers of Tomorrow*, The Association of Writers for National Literature, 2011.

K-픽션 019
어느 피씨주의자의 종생기

2017년 10월 30일 초판 1쇄 발행

**지은이** 구병모 | **옮긴이** 스텔라 김 | **펴낸이** 김재범
**기획위원** 전성태, 정은경, 이경재
**편집** 김형욱, 신아름 | **관리** 강초민, 홍희표 | **디자인** 나루기획
**인쇄·제책** AP프린팅 | **종이** 한솔PNS
**펴낸곳**(주)아시아 | **출판등록** 2006년 1월 27일 제406-2006-000004호
**주소** 경기도 파주시 회동길 445(서울 사무소: 서울특별시 동작구 서달로 161-1 3층)
**전화** 02.821.5055 | **팩스** 02.821.5057 | **홈페이지** www.bookasia.org
ISBN 979-11-5662-173-7(set) | 979-11-5662-332-8(04810)
값은 뒤표지에 있습니다.

K-Fiction 019
The Story of P.C.

**Written by** Gu Byeong-mo | **Translated by** Stella Kim
**Published by** ASIA Publishers | 445, Hoedong-gil, Paju-si, Gyeonggi-do, Korea
(Seoul Office:161-1, Seodal-ro, Dongjak-gu, Seoul, Korea)
**Homepage Address** www.bookasia.org | **Tel.**(822).821.5055 | **Fax.**(822).821.5057
First published in Korea by ASIA Publishers 2017
ISBN 979-11-5662-173-7(set) | 979-11-5662-332-8(04810)

## 바이링궐 에디션 한국 대표 소설

한국문학의 가장 중요하고 첨예한 문제의식을 가진 작가들의 대표작을 주제별로 선정!
하버드 한국학 연구원 및 세계 각국의 한국문학 전문 번역진이 참여한 번역 시리즈!
미국 하버드대학교와 컬럼비아대학교 동아시아학과, 캐나다 브리티시컬럼비아대학교 아시아학과 등 해외 대학에서 교재로 채택!

### 바이링궐 에디션 한국 대표 소설 set 1

**분단** Division

01 병신과 머저리-**이청준** The Wounded-**Yi Cheong-jun**
02 어둠의 혼-**김원일** Soul of Darkness-**Kim Won-il**
03 순이삼촌-**현기영** Sun-i Samch'on-**Hyun Ki-young**
04 엄마의 말뚝 1-**박완서** Mother's Stake I-**Park Wan-suh**
05 유형의 땅-**조정래** The Land of the Banished-**Jo Jung-rae**

**산업화** Industrialization

06 무진기행-**김승옥** Record of a Journey to Mujin-**Kim Seung-ok**
07 삼포 가는 길-**황석영** The Road to Sampo-**Hwang Sok-yong**
08 아홉 켤레의 구두로 남은 사내-**윤흥길** The Man Who Was Left as Nine Pairs of Shoes-**Yun Heung-gil**
09 돌아온 우리의 친구-**신상웅** Our Friend's Homecoming-**Shin Sang-ung**
10 원미동 시인-**양귀자** The Poet of Wŏnmi-dong-**Yang Kwi-ja**

**여성** Women

11 중국인 거리-**오정희** Chinatown-**Oh Jung-hee**
12 풍금이 있던 자리-**신경숙** The Place Where the Harmonium Was-**Shin Kyung-sook**
13 하나코는 없다-**최윤** The Last of Hanak'o-**Ch'oe Yun**
14 인간에 대한 예의-**공지영** Human Decency-**Gong Ji-young**
15 빈처-**은희경** Poor Man's Wife-**Eun Hee-kyung**

### 바이링궐 에디션 한국 대표 소설 set 2

**자유** Liberty

16 필론의 돼지-**이문열** Pilon's Pig-**Yi Mun-yol**
17 슬로우 불릿-**이대환** Slow Bullet-**Lee Dae-hwan**
18 직선과 독가스-**임철우** Straight Lines and Poison Gas-**Lim Chul-woo**
19 깃발-**홍희담** The Flag-**Hong Hee-dam**
20 새벽 출정-**방현석** Off to Battle at Dawn-**Bang Hyeon-seok**

**사랑과 연애 Love and Love Affairs**

21 별을 사랑하는 마음으로-**윤후명** With the Love for the Stars-**Yun Hu-myong**
22 목련공원-**이승우** Magnolia Park-**Lee Seung-u**
23 칼에 찔린 자국-**김인숙** Stab-**Kim In-suk**
24 회복하는 인간-**한강** Convalescence-**Han Kang**
25 트렁크-**정이현** In the Trunk-**Jeong Yi-hyun**

**남과 북 South and North**

26 판문점-**이호철** Panmunjom-**Yi Ho-chol**
27 수난 이대-**하근찬** The Suffering of Two Generations-**Ha Geun-chan**
28 분지-**남정현** Land of Excrement-**Nam Jung-hyun**
29 봄 실상사-**정도상** Spring at Silsangsa Temple-**Jeong Do-sang**
30 은행나무 사랑-**김하기** Gingko Love-**Kim Ha-kee**

## 바이링궐 에디션 한국 대표 소설 set 3

**서울 Seoul**

31 눈사람 속의 검은 항아리-**김소진** The Dark Jar within the Snowman-**Kim So-jin**
32 오후, 가로지르다-**하성란** Traversing Afternoon-**Ha Seong-nan**
33 나는 봉천동에 산다-**조경란** I Live in Bongcheon-dong-**Jo Kyung-ran**
34 그렇습니까? 기린입니다-**박민규** Is That So? I'm A Giraffe-**Park Min-gyu**
35 성탄특선-**김애란** Christmas Specials-**Kim Ae-ran**

**전통 Tradition**

36 무자년의 가을 사흘-**서정인** Three Days of Autumn, 1948-**Su Jung-in**
37 유자소전-**이문구** A Brief Biography of Yuja-**Yi Mun-gu**
38 향기로운 우물 이야기-**박범신** The Fragrant Well-**Park Bum-shin**
39 월행-**송기원** A Journey under the Moonlight-**Song Ki-won**
40 협죽도 그늘 아래-**성석제** In the Shade of the Oleander-**Song Sok-ze**

**아방가르드 Avant-garde**

41 아겔다마-**박상륭** Akeldama-**Park Sang-ryoong**
42 내 영혼의 우물-**최인석** A Well in My Soul-**Choi In-seok**
43 당신에 대해서-**이인성** On You-**Yi In-seong**
44 회색 時-**배수아** Time In Gray-**Bae Su-ah**
45 브라운 부인-**정영문** Mrs. Brown-**Jung Young-moon**

## 바이링궐 에디션 한국 대표 소설 set 4

**디아스포라 Diaspora**

46 속옷-**김남일** Underwear-**Kim Nam-il**
47 상하이에 두고 온 사람들-**공선옥** People I Left in Shanghai-**Gong Sun-ok**
48 모두에게 복된 새해-**김연수** Happy New Year to Everyone-**Kim Yeon-su**
49 코끼리-**김재영** The Elephant-**Kim Jae-young**
50 먼지별-**이경** Dust Star-**Lee Kyung**

**가족 Family**

51 혜자의 눈꽃-**천승세** Hye-ja's Snow-Flowers-**Chun Seung-sei**
52 아베의 가족-**전상국** Ahbe's Family-**Jeon Sang-guk**
53 문 앞에서-**이동하** Outside the Door-**Lee Dong-ha**
54 그리고, 축제-**이혜경** And Then the Festival-**Lee Hye-kyung**
55 봄밤-**권여선** Spring Night-**Kwon Yeo-sun**

**유머 Humor**

56 오늘의 운세-**한창훈** Today's Fortune-**Han Chang-hoon**
57 새-**전성태** Bird-**Jeon Sung-tae**
58 밀수록 다시 가까워지는-**이기호** So Far, and Yet So Near-**Lee Ki-ho**
59 유리방패-**김중혁** The Glass Shield-**Kim Jung-hyuk**
60 전당포를 찾아서-**김종광** The Pawnshop Chase-**Kim Chong-kwang**

## 바이링궐 에디션 한국 대표 소설 set 5

**관계 Relationship**

61 도둑견습 – **김주영** Robbery Training-**Kim Joo-young**
62 사랑하라, 희망 없이 – **윤영수** Love, Hopelessly-**Yun Young-su**
63 봄날 오후, 과부 셋 – **정지아** Spring Afternoon, Three Widows-**Jeong Ji-a**
64 유턴 지점에 보물지도를 묻다 - **윤성희** Burying a Treasure Map at the U-turn-**Yoon Sung-hee**
65 쁘이거나 쯔이거나 - **백가흠** Puy, Thuy, Whatever-**Paik Ga-huim**

**일상의 발견 Discovering Everyday Life**

66 나는 음식이다 – **오수연** I Am Food-**Oh Soo-yeon**
67 트럭 – **강영숙** Truck-**Kang Young-sook**
68 통조림 공장 - **편혜영** The Canning Factory-**Pyun Hye-young**
69 꽃 – **부희령** Flowers-**Pu Hee-ryoung**
70 피의일요일 – **윤이형** Bloody Sunday-**Yun I-hyeong**

**금기와 욕망 Taboo and Desire**

71 북소리 - **송영** Drumbeat-**Song Yong**
72 발칸의 장미를 내게 주었네 - **정미경** He Gave Me Roses of the Balkans-**Jung Mi-kyung**
73 아무도 돌아오지 않는 밤 – **김숨** The Night Nobody Returns Home-**Kim Soom**
74 젓가락여자 – **천운영** Chopstick Woman-**Cheon Un-yeong**
75 아직 일어나지 않은 일 – **김미월** What Has Yet to Happen-**Kim Mi-wol**

## 바이링궐 에디션 한국 대표 소설 set 6

**운명 Fate**

76 언니를 놓치다 – **이경자** Losing a Sister-**Lee Kyung-ja**
77 아들 – **윤정모** Father and Son-**Yoon Jung-mo**
78 명두 – **구효서** Relics-**Ku Hyo-seo**
79 모독 – **조세희** Insult-**Cho Se-hui**
80 화요일의 강 – **손홍규** Tuesday River-**Son Hong-gyu**

**미의 사제들 Aesthetic Priests**

81 고수 – **이외수** Grand Master-**Lee Oisoo**
82 말을 찾아서 – **이순원** Looking for a Horse-**Lee Soon-won**
83 상춘곡 – **윤대녕** Song of Everlasting Spring-**Youn Dae-nyeong**
84 삭매와 자미 – **김별아** Sakmae and Jami-**Kim Byeol-ah**
85 저만치 혼자서 – **김훈** Alone Over There-**Kim Hoon**

**식민지의 벌거벗은 자들 The Naked in the Colony**

86 감자 – **김동인** Potatoes-**Kim Tong-in**
87 운수 좋은 날 – **현진건** A Lucky Day-**Hyŏn Chin'gŏn**
88 탈출기 – **최서해** Escape-**Ch'oe So-hae**
89 과도기 – **한설야** Transition-**Han Seol-ya**
90 지하촌 – **강경애** The Underground Village-**Kang Kyŏng-ae**

## 바이링궐 에디션 한국 대표 소설 set 7

**백치가 된 식민지 지식인 Colonial Intellectuals Turned "Idiots"**

91 날개 – **이상** Wings-**Yi Sang**
92 김 강사와 T 교수 – **유진오** Lecturer Kim and Professor T-**Chin-O Yu**
93 소설가 구보씨의 일일 – **박태원** A Day in the Life of Kubo the Novelist-**Pak Taewon**
94 비 오는 길 – **최명익** Walking in the Rain-**Ch'oe Myŏngik**
95 빛 속에 – **김사량** Into the Light-**Kim Sa-ryang**

**한국의 잃어버린 얼굴 Traditional Korea's Lost Faces**

96 봄·봄 – **김유정** Spring, Spring–**Kim Yu-jeong**
97 벙어리 삼룡이 – **나도향** Samnyong the Mute–**Na Tohyang**
98 달밤 – **이태준** An Idiot's Delight–**Yi T'ae-jun**
99 사랑손님과 어머니 – **주요섭** Mama and the Boarder–**Chu Yo-sup**
100 갯마을 – **오영수** Seaside Village–**Oh Yeongsu**

**해방 전후(前後) Before and After Liberation**

101 소망 – **채만식** Juvesenility–**Ch'ae Man-Sik**
102 두 파산 – **염상섭** Two Bankruptcies–**Yom Sang-Seop**
103 풀잎 – **이효석** Leaves of Grass–**Lee Hyo-seok**
104 맥 – **김남천** Barley–**Kim Namch'on**
105 꺼삐딴 리 – **전광용** Kapitan Ri–**Chŏn Kwangyong**

**전후(戰後) Korea After the Korean War**

106 소나기 – **황순원** The Cloudburst–**Hwang Sun-Won**
107 등신불 – **김동리** Tŭngsin-bul–**Kim Tong-ni**
108 요한 시집 – **장용학** The Poetry of John–**Chang Yong-hak**
109 비 오는 날 – **손창섭** Rainy Days–**Son Chang-sop**
110 오발탄 – **이범선** A Stray Bullet–**Lee Beomseon**

## K-픽션 한국 젊은 소설

최근에 발표된 단편소설 중 가장 우수하고 흥미로운 작품을 엄선하여 출간하는 <K-픽션>은 한국문학의 생생한 현장을 국내외 독자들과 실시간으로 공유하고자 기획되었습니다. 원작의 재미와 품격을 최대한 살린 <K-픽션> 시리즈는 매 계절마다 새로운 작품을 선보입니다.

001 버핏과의 저녁 식사-**박민규** Dinner with Buffett-**Park Min-gyu**
002 아르판-**박형서** Arpan-**Park hyoung su**
003 애드벌룬-**손보미** Hot Air Balloon-**Son Bo-mi**
004 나의 클린트 이스트우드-**오한기** My Clint Eastwood-**Oh Han-ki**
005 이베리아의 전갈-**최민우** Dishonored-**Choi Min-woo**
006 양의 미래-**황정은** Kong's Garden-**Hwang Jung-eun**
007 대니-**윤이형** Danny-**Yun I-hyeong**
008 퇴근-**천명관** Homecoming-**Cheon Myeong-kwan**
009 옥화-**금희** Ok-hwa-**Geum Hee**
010 시차-**백수린** Time Difference-**Baik Sou linne**
011 올드 맨 리버-**이장욱** Old Man River-**Lee Jang-wook**
012 권순찬과 착한 사람들-**이기호** Kwon Sun-chan and Nice People-**Lee Ki-ho**
013 알바생 자르기-**장강명** Fired-**Chang Kangmyoung**
014 어디로 가고 싶으신가요-**김애란** Where Would You Like To Go?-**Kim Ae-ran**
015 세상에서 가장 비싼 소설-**김민정** The World's Most Expensive Novel-**Kim Min-jung**
016 체스의 모든 것-**김금희** Everything About Chess-**Kim Keum-hee**
017 할로윈-**정한아** Halloween-**Chung Han-ah**
018 그 여름-**최은영** The Summer-**Choi Eunyoung**
019 어느 피씨주의자의 종생기-**구병모** The Story of P.C.-**Gu Byeong-mo**